THE LONG TRAIL

Texas Ranger Mike Hart rode back to Amarillo after successfully capturing Buck Radd, the notorious bank robber. But then he learned that Radd had already been busted out of the jail where he was awaiting trial, and was again robbing banks and committing murder. He rode back to where Radd had been operating, facing ambush and cold-blooded killing. And as he courageously pushed on, his exceptional talents were hard pressed — right to the last shot . . .

CORBA SUNMAN

THE LONG TRAIL

Complete and Unabridged

LINFORD
Leicester

First published in Great Britain in 2007 by
Robert Hale Limited
London

First Linford Edition
published 2008
by arrangement with
Robert Hale Limited
London

British Library CIP Data

Sunman, Corba
  The long trail.—Large print ed.—
  Linford western library
  1. Western stories
  2. Large type books
  I. Title
  823.9′2 [F]

  ISBN 978–1–84782–207–9

Published by
F. A. Thorpe (Publishing)
Anstey, Leicestershire

Set by Words & Graphics Ltd.
Anstey, Leicestershire
Printed and bound in Great Britain by
T. J. International Ltd., Padstow, Cornwall

This book is printed on acid-free paper

1

Amarillo was sweltering in the heat of high summer when Mike Hart rode into town and headed for the adobe brick office of the local Texas Rangers headquarters. He left his black stallion at a tie-rack and crossed the sidewalk to the door of the office, smiling in anticipation of seeing Captain Ed Buckbee again. Entering the office, he paused to allow his eyes to adjust to the dim light pervading the interior. Buckbee was seated at a board table by an open window; his shirt-sleeves rolled up and an expression of harassment on his weathered face.

Buckbee, startled by Hart's sudden entrance, hastily pocketed a magnifying glass he had been using. In his middle-fifties, he had discovered that the onset of old age eroded the sharp edges of a man's abilities, and he was

1

shy of letting anyone discover that he could not see as well as he had even ten years before. Short in stature, and now showing signs of running to fat, he had gained his awesome reputation against the bad men of Texas thirty years before. His brown eyes were serious as he looked up at Hart.

'Howdy, Cap'n.' Hart frowned as he saw the unmistakable signs of his superior slipping into old age — greying hair thinning and turning white at the temples. 'I got here fast as I could. What's cooking now? I was hoping for a few days off duty. You're sure working me hard this year.'

'Mike, my hair has been turning grey waiting for you to show up.' Buckbee took in Hart's tall, powerfully built figure, his gaze critical, and a pang of sadness cut through his breast at the sight of Hart's obvious youth, which took him back thirty years in his thoughts. 'You look OK after tangling with Buck Radd. I read your report from Larchville with great interest. It didn't take you long to put Radd behind bars and bust up his crooked business. He was facing twenty years in prison for that string of bank-robberies he committed, but while you were heading back here, someone busted him out of the jail back in Bleak Ridge. He's running free again, and you're gonna have to start over. Apparently you missed some of his gang in the clean-up. Sheriff Bland reports that Ike Gotch, one of Radd's top gunnies, led the rescue gang.'

Hart stifled a groan and slapped a hand against his thigh. 'Damn! I knew I should have planted Radd permanent when I had the chance. I got a sneaking feeling I was doing wrong, toting him in for trial.'

'No.' Buckbee shook his head. 'You did right. It was Sheriff Bland made the mistake, and now you've got to ride that trail again. I have a report telling me that a man answering Radd's description led four men into the bank in Garfield yesterday afternoon and

3

lifted four thousand dollars. They got clean away, leaving two dead clerks in the bank — shot down in cold blood.'

'Garfield is seventy-odd miles from Bleak Ridge. Did Radd have time to get there?'

'Yeah. It all ties in. It was Radd all right. Sheriff Bland has two posses out, but if Radd's past record is anything to go by, they won't see hide or hair of the outlaws. Head back to Bleak Ridge, and this time shoot Radd in his legs, if you take him alive, so anyone busting him out of jail again will have to carry him. But getting Radd is only secondary to the job that's just come up, Mike. Look for Radd by all means, but if he's gone to earth you'll have trouble digging him out again, so leave him be till later. I've got a report of trouble down San Fedora way. You're going back to Bleak Ridge, so when you get the chance, drop in at the Double S south of San Fedora and talk to Sam Straker. He's a great friend of mine — we rode together in the early days of the

4

Rangers — and I know he wouldn't complain unless there was big trouble on his plate.'

'OK, Cap'n, I'll hit the trail in about ten minutes. I need some supplies and a couple of boxes of cartridges, and mebbe I can take the time to refill my canteen, huh?'

'Sure.' Buckbee grinned. 'Take all the time you need, but be outa town within ten minutes. Don't forget to keep me informed of your progress. You're getting a mite slack with your reports. I'm sitting around this danged office for days on end, waiting for news, while you're riding over half of Texas enjoying yourself.'

Hart grinned, and his blue eyes glinted as he turned to the door. 'Be seeing you, Cap'n,' he said, and departed.

True to his word, Hart was riding out of town minutes later, heading south towards the border country, and he paused to take a wistful last look at the clustered buildings of the town. He had been looking forward to a break from law-dealing, if only for a couple of days, but Captain Buckbee was a hard taskmaster, and he turned resolutely to the waiting trail and touched spurs to the big black stallion. Unfinished business lay ahead, and he was determined to write *finis* to the vicious career of Buck Radd . . .

* * *

Two weeks of steady riding brought Hart to the outskirts of Bleak Ridge and he let the black walk into the main street as he headed for the sheriff's office. His keen gaze took in the stark details of the town as he dismounted and trailed the black's reins. Nothing had changed in the weeks since he had left Buck Radd here in jail awaiting trial, but he was keenly aware that the big investigation he had made, which culminated in the end of the unlawful activities of Radd, had been a waste of time because the outlaw was free to continue his vicious trail of robbery and murder.

The door of the law office was locked, and Hart peered through the big front window to see that the place was deserted. He frowned as he surveyed the unusually quiet street, for he needed to get reports from the local law before renewing his investigation.

A sigh escaped Hart as he led his black along the street to the livery barn. Taking care of the animal's needs was a priority, and when he was satisfied that Blackie was comfortable he carried his saddle-bags and Winchester as he retraced his steps along the street. The Longhorn saloon attracted him and he shouldered through the batwing doors and walked to the bar, his spurs tinkling. He dumped his saddle-bags on the bar and beckoned to the 'tender, who was engaged in conversation with the solitary patron bellied up to the bar. The silence in the big room, which was usually busy at this late hour, was over-powering.

'Gimme a beer, Charlie,' Hart called, and the bartender came scurrying towards him, a grin of welcome on his smooth face. 'What's going on?' he asked. 'The town is quieter than Boot Hill on a Sunday evening. Where is everybody?'

'The sheriff is running two posses.' The 'tender's fleshy face pulled into a grimace as he placed a glass of beer before Hart. He was short and fat, balding, and his dark eyes flickered nervously as he spoke. 'They've been going at it for weeks now, chasing shadows all the way to the border and back in their search for Radd and his gang. Tom Bland sure is het up at the way Radd escaped from jail, and he ain't sparing any efforts to recapture him. But anyone can see he's wasting his time. No one could catch Radd before you got him, and now he's free again, thumbing his nose at the law despite the sheriff's efforts.'

Hart lifted the glass of beer and drained it as he digested the barman's words. He set down the empty glass.

'Who's running the law in town while the posses are out?' he asked, pushing back his Stetson to wipe sweat from his forehead.

'Bull Santee, but he's never on duty around town when the sheriff is away.'

'Santee, huh?' Hart nodded, recalling his dislike of the massive deputy when they had met on his previous visit. 'Any idea where he hangs out when he's not in the law office?'

'Rosita, one of our saloon gals, has a cabin on the back lot behind the saloon. You'll likely find Santee with her, if you wanta see him real bad. If you ask me, the sheriff made a bad mistake leaving Santee in the big saddle.'

'What makes you say that?'

Charlie Bain shrugged and grimaced. 'It ain't for me to say. Santee would love to have an excuse to beat me up. He's too fond of using his fists to settle arguments; they don't call him Bull for nothing. He never was much as a deputy, but he seems to be getting worse these days.'

'I noticed his bullying ways when I was here before.' Hart nodded. 'Take care of my saddle-bags and Winchester, Charlie. I need to talk to Santee pronto.'

He turned away, left by the rear door of the saloon, and emerged on to the back lots, where several cabins and shacks dotted the stark landscape. He crossed to the nearest cabin and rapped on the door, his thoughts busy as he awaited a reply.

The door was opened by a slim, dark-haired girl, whose dusky features indicated her Mexican ancestry. She was pretty, but her looks were marred by a swelling around her left eye, and there was a gash on her forehead over the eyebrow.

'Howdy, Rosita,' Hart greeted. 'Who declared war on you?'

'Señor Hart, you're back.' Relief surged into the girl's expression. 'I heard you were coming. I need your help to get that fat pig, Bull Santee, out of my cabin. Please make him stay away from me. I can't take any more of his bullying. If you can't help me then I'll stick a knife in him, so help me.'

'Hey, Rosita, what in hell is going on now?' The heavy voice emanating from inside the cabin was laced with bad humour. 'Get back in here and fix my grub. I got to be in the saloon shortly. Make it quick or I'll smack your other eye.'

Rosita sighed and looked plaintively at Hart.

'Please,' she begged. 'Help me.'

Hart grasped the girl's arm and moved her out of the doorway. He entered the cabin to find Santee sprawled on a bed in a corner. The interior reeked of stale whiskey and cigarette smoke. Hart crossed to the bed, grasped Santee by his shirt-front, lifted him bodily from the bed and thrust him towards the door. Santee cursed and raised hamlike fists. He was a head taller than Hart, and heavily muscled. His bull neck supported a large head. His features were coarse, his black hair uncombed, and matted, and his dark eyes were wild with exploding anger.

'What the hell!' he roared. 'What in hell is going on?' His eyes were bleary and he was unsteady on his feet. Reeking of whiskey fumes and blinking owlishly, he threw a right-hand punch at Hart that would have laid the Ranger low if it had connected.

Hart swayed his head away from the clubbing right fist and set his feet solidly on the floor. Holding Santee by the shirt-front, he loosed his big left fist in a whirling hook that smacked solidly against the big man's jaw. Santee's knees gave way instantly, and Hart grasped the seat of Santee's pants and gave him the bum's rush out of the cabin. He released his hold on the deputy and Santee sprawled on his face in the dirt, puffing and blowing like a rooting hog as dust rose around his tousled head. Hart dusted his hands together as he awaited Santee's next move.

'I knew you could do it!' Rosita smiled, enjoying the sight of Santee's discomfiture, 'but can you make him stay away from me?'

'It ain't over yet, not by a long rope, but he'll get the message by the time he's had enough,' Hart replied.

Santee came up off the ground like a wild bull, snorting and cursing. He threw himself at Hart, head down and fists whirling. Hart deflected a massive right and threw a left hook that smacked against Santee's chin. The blow pulled Santee up short and he tottered. Hart hit him with a solid right under the heart that put springs into Santee's legs. The big man wavered, lost his balance, and went over backwards like a tree uprooted in a storm.

Hart waited, and was faintly surprised when Santee came upright again, but the deputy's hands remained at waist level and he looked around blearily, as if his sight had failed him.

'I'm here,' Hart said crisply as Santee

tottered around on unsteady legs.

Santee blinked and shook his head. Blood was dribbling from his mouth and he spat. He came forward an uncertain pace, guided by Hart's voice, and Hart hit him with another jolting right that dumped him back on the ground on the seat of his pants. He tried to rise yet again but the effort was beyond him. He fell back and lay gasping for breath, his arms wide and his mouth agape.

Rosita clapped her hands. 'That was a real beating!' she exclaimed 'But you will have to watch your back now, because Santee cannot take a beating. Can't you find an excuse to shoot him, Señor Hart?'

'I'll throw him in jail if he won't leave you alone, Rosita. Tell me what's been going on around here since I left. Do you know how Buck Radd escaped?'

'Someone passed a gun to him and he shot Deputy Wilkes before walking out of the jail. A horse was ready-saddled along the street, and Radd just rode out of town.'

'Is that a fact?' Hart frowned as he considered.

Santee was beginning to stir. Hart watched the big deputy for a couple of moments, then reached down and grasped Santee's shirt. He hauled the man to his feet and supported him. Santee was hung over. His weight dragged against Hart's hand. He was breathing heavily. His eyelids fluttered. Blood dribbled from his swollen mouth.

'Come on, Santee,' Hart rapped unsympathetically. 'Stand on your own two feet I heard tell you were tough all ways to the middle, but you just can't fight worth chicken-feed. You should give up law dealing and take a job cleaning out the livery barn.'

He released his grasp on the deputy's shirt and stepped back a pace. Santee swayed, and had to move his feet quickly to maintain his balance. He straightened and opened his eyes fully to glare at Hart with the ferocity and frustration of a caged mountain lion.

'What in hell did you hit me for?' he demanded. 'I was minding my own business. How come you're back here again? What in hell do you want?'

'Buck Radd,' Hart said. 'So tell me how he got out of jail?'

'I got no idea.' Santee shook his head. 'I wasn't even in town the night he escaped. I'd gone over to Campville for a couple of days.'

'So you heard afterwards that Radd had escaped. Any idea who passed the gun to him through the bars?'

'Nope. The sheriff reckoned someone sneaked up to the rear of the jail and slipped it through the back window, which looks into the cell Radd occupied. Radd waited till after supper when Wilkes was alone, got the drop on him, and killed him before leaving. There was a horse waiting ready-saddled along the street and Radd vanished. No one's seen hide or hair of him since, but he pulled off a couple robberies south of here, and more men have been killed.'

'And the sheriff is wasting his time riding around the country like a scalded cat, huh?' Hart shook his head. 'I guess Bland's pride was hurt, but he won't get Radd by chasing over the country following whispers. How come you were left here looking after the town? Doesn't the sheriff know you're a no-good? I wouldn't trust you to run a Sunday school!'

Santee shrugged. 'You wanta know anything else?' he demanded. 'If not, I'll head for the law office.'

'I heard you say you wanted to be in the saloon,' Hart rebuked. 'You better straighten yourself out, Santee, or you'll be out of a job, and that's the truth. And stay away from Rosita. You lay a hand on her again and I'll teach you a lesson you won't ever forget.'

'Me and Rosita go back a long way,' Santee blustered. 'She can't complain about me.'

'I want nothing more to do with you,' Rosita cut in. 'Stay away from me, Santee. You're a pig! I don't want you

17

coming here again. If I see you I'll call for Señor Hart.'

Santee sneered and turned away. He staggered towards the rear of the saloon, and Hart watched the deputy's wavering progress until he lurched into the building and slammed the back door.

'Let me know if you have any more trouble with him, Rosita,' Hart said. 'He's a no-good. I'm wondering why you picked up with him in the first place.'

'I didn't,' Rosita protested. 'He picked me. I didn't get the chance to say no to him. Thank you for stepping in, *señor*. You're a good man.'

Hart smiled and went back to the street. He went along the sidewalk to an eating-house, assuaged his hunger, and afterwards went into the hotel to take a room. Then he went along to the saloon to collect his saddle-bags and rifle.

Santee was still in the saloon, leaning against the bar, a glass of whiskey before him. Charlie Bain, the 'tender, grimaced at Hart when he entered.

'Hey, Hart, no hard feelings,' Santee called. 'What's your poison?'

'I'm not drinking,' Hart replied. 'Gimme my gear, Charlie.'

Bain produced Hart's saddle-bags and rifle and laid them on the bar top.

'Goin' hunting Buck Radd?' Santee drawled. 'I hope you've got better luck than the sheriff right now. Bland ain't been in his office more than a few minutes in the past month. Radd is running rings around him, and thumbing his nose at the law.'

'Radd is on a short rope,' Hart replied. 'I'll haul him in again when I'm ready. I'm more interested right now in who busted him out of the jail.'

Santee sniggered. 'He's got a lot of friends in these parts. You'll be wasting your time hunting him, just like the sheriff.'

Hart picked up his gear and left the saloon. He paused to look around the deserted street. Most of the townsmen were out with the two posses. A rider was coming into town, and Hart studied the lone figure from force of habit, his hunting instincts working incessantly.

The newcomer cantered along the street, and reined up in front of the general store. Hart watched him dismount, and his interest sharpened suddenly for there was something familiar in the appearance of the man that struck a chord in his mind. Hart narrowed his gaze, and as the stranger crossed the sidewalk to enter the store it came to him with the force of a thunderbolt. He was looking at Ike Gotch, a prominent member of the Buck Radd gang!

Hart eased sideways into an alley mouth. What was Gotch doing here in Bleak Ridge when two posses were out scouring the country for the gang? He craned forward and looked both ways along the wide, rutted street, half-expecting to see other members of the gang appearing. Had Radd made plans to hit the bank here in town while the place was deserted?

Two riders were coming along the street from the same direction Gotch had appeared. Hart dropped his saddle-bags, stood his rifle against a wall, and drew his pistol to check the big weapon. The two riders reined in across the street from the bank and dismounted to stand with their horses — one of them apparently absorbed with his saddle-bags.

The click of hoofs from the opposite direction caught Hart's ears and he craned forward to see two riders emerging from an alley on the other side of the saloon to come riding casually towards the bank. Hart eased back as they approached his position, and realized, as they passed, that one of them was Buck Radd. He knew most of the gang by sight, and found himself marvelling at Radd's audacity, and yet the gang boss would never have a better opportunity of robbing the bank in Bleak Ridge than when the sheriff and most of the able-bodied men were out of town.

Hart drew a deep breath. His heart was pounding and pressure built up in his breast to an intolerable degree. He had been this close to Radd only once before, and that was when he arrested the gang boss. Now Radd was here in town, unaware that the man he most feared was watching from a position of vantage, ready to take a hand in the action that was surely coming up. Hart grinned, dispelling his tension, liking the thought of getting Radd at a disadvantage.

Radd and his sidekick made straight for the bank and dismounted in front of the door. The two men opposite the bank suddenly crossed the street to join Radd, and Hart saw Ike Gotch appear in the doorway of the store, glance around the street, and then take up his reins to lead his horse across the street to the bank. One man stayed with the horses while Radd led the others across the sidewalk and into the bank.

Hart checked his pistol and then

cocked it. He stepped out of the alley-mouth and moved diagonally across the street towards the bank, He had covered half the distance when he was spotted by the outlaw holding the gang's horses. The man immediately drew his holstered six-gun. Hart triggered his Colt. The crash of the shot wrecked the silence overhanging the town, and echoes grumbled away into the distance as the outlaw jerked and then spun around to fall heavily.

The waiting horses moved restlessly, and two of them set off at a gallop away along the street. The door of the bank opened and the outlaws emerged in a rush, drawn guns blasting at the lone figure of Hart standing in the centre of the street. Hart returned fire, dropping to one knee to lessen his target area. The foremost outlaw came off the sidewalk like a drunken man and pitched on to his face in the dust. Hart looked for the big figure of Buck Radd, wanting to nail the gang boss, but at that moment he was dealt a ferocious blow on the left side of his head which sent his Stetson whirling and flattened him into the dust.

His last conscious thought was that he had been shot from behind . . .

2

When Hart opened his eyes he found himself lying on his back in the street with the tall, thin figure of Doc Elmore bending over him. His head was aching intolerably but his senses were clear and he could remember every instant of what had occurred immediately before he had been tagged by a bullet from behind. He lifted probing fingers to the left side of his head and felt the stickiness of blood before Elmore pushed his hand away.

'Lie still while I treat you,' Elmore said. 'You're a very lucky man. A bullet took some hair and skin off your head on the left side just above and behind the ear. I've heard tell of such wounds, but this is the first time I've come across one. I expect you have a headache, but your eyes are clear so I don't think you'll have any bad lasting effects.'

'What's happened to the bank robbers?' Hart demanded. 'I recognized the Radd gang.'

'They've gone now, and there's one of them dead in the street. Henry Damon told me they took more than two thousand dollars out of his bank, and one of his tellers was shot dead.'

Hart groaned as he pushed himself into a sitting position. He looked around to see a crowd which was composed mainly of women, gathered in front of the bank. A supine figure was lying in the dust in front of the bank, toes upturned and arms outflung. The doctor grasped Hart's arm and helped him to his feet. For a moment the whole street seemed to tilt, and Hart closed his eyes, but the bad moment passed. He drew a deep breath and forced himself to take stock of the situation.

He crossed to where the dead robber was lying and recognized Tom Oakie, a well-known member of the Radd gang. He looked at the open door of the bank and saw Santee standing on the threshold, talking seriously to someone who was out of Hart's sight. Hart crossed the sidewalk and peered into the bank. Santee was talking to Henry Damon, the banker. A man was lying dead on the floor with blood on his shirt-front.

'It was Radd and his bunch,' Santee said when he looked round at Hart, 'They got away with a lot of dough.'

'Tell me something I don't know,' Hart replied. 'I killed Oakie. He was holding their horses, and I would have got more of the gang if I hadn't been tagged by a slug.' He paused and lifted a hand to his head. The bullet had struck him from behind. 'Where were you when the shooting started, Santee?'

'In the saloon. I came out to the street when I heard the first shot, and saw you down in the dust and Radd and the rest of his bunch heading out of town I sent some slugs after them but they kept riding.'

'Did you see anyone at my back?'

Hart demanded. 'I was shot from behind.' He paused and studied Santee's coarse face as a thought struck him. 'Did one of your shots clip me, Santee?'

'Like hell! You were down when I came on the scene. One of the robbers might have been back along the street to cover the gang's rear, and he could have ridden out in the opposite direction so you didn't see him.'

Hart heaved a sigh. He had a sneaking suspicion that Santee had shot him, probably deliberately, and made a note to check out the deputy's movements.

'So Radd took the chance of coming in here while all the townsmen were out with the posses,' he observed. 'The sheriff won't be happy about that.'

'He's been chasing after Radd too long,' Damon grumbled. 'His first duty is to the town, and if he'd been doing his job properly Radd wouldn't have come in here like he did. He's got a nerve, riding in as if he owned the place. And Frank is dead — shot down in cold blood!'

Hart looked down at the inert bank teller. Radd had made killing a teller a trade mark on his recent raids. He sighed and turned away.

'I'll split the breeze,' he said. 'Tell the sheriff I'm on Radd's trail, huh? I'll come back and report to him when I can.'

He went out to the street and looked at hoof-prints. The tracks were deep and fresh, and he followed them along the street as far as the livery barn. He saddled his black stallion and rode out of town at a canter, his gaze bent upon the tell-tale marks that he hoped would lead him eventually to Radd and his crooked bunch.

Hart had planned to stick around Bleak Ridge for a few days to give his horse a rest but the initiative had been taken from him and he urged the black along at its best pace, fully aware that the animal was sluggish from its exertions over the past month. But tracks were plain upon the ground and he considered the options open to Radd as he followed at a lope.

During his operation to catch Radd the first time, Hart had learned a great deal about the gang boss. Buck Radd was a callous man who spilled blood indiscriminately on his numerous raids. Witnesses stated that bank tellers in particular had been gunned down in cold blood, and gang members had begun following their leader's grim pattern of behaviour, their exploits making them one of the most vicious gangs operating in Texas.

Hart pondered on Radd's escape from the Bleak Ridge jail, suspecting that someone in the town had been responsible for the gun that had found its way into the hands of the murderous gang boss, but he kept an open mind on the subject, for any one of the gang could have sneaked in under the cover of darkness to provide Radd with the means of escape. They were an audacious bunch with no human qualities in their make-up.

The tracks led off into the south-west, and Radd was moving fast. Hart let his mind rove ahead of the trail, wondering at the gang leader's ultimate goal. Radd would want to drop out of sight, which meant riding into some border town to spend his ill-gotten gains and then lying low until the need for more money galvanized the crooked bunch into further action.

The gang itself numbered around ten men who each had a bad reputation. Ike Gotch, Radd's right-hand man, was wanted for several murders, and the faces of most of the other members of the gang appeared on wanted posters all over Texas. The Texas Rangers had gone all out to capture the gang, but even their great efforts had been to no avail. Radd had many friends all over the south-west, and they spared no efforts to help the bank robber.

Hart figured that the tracks of the gang were heading towards the distant town of Broken Hill. He set a faster pace, and was ten miles from Bleak Ridge when a rifle shot split the heavy silence and sent echoes grumbling towards the horizon. He reined in quickly but did not reach for his pistol because he had not heard the sound of closely passing lead. He spotted a group of riders way off to his left and sat his mount, watching their approach.

He recognized the big figure of Sheriff Bland leading the dozen or so hard-faced riders long before they reached him, and noted their trail-weary condition as they came up. Bland was a middle-aged man, probably near to fifty, and his dusty face showed bitter lines of defeat as he reined in. His blue eyes were narrowed against the glare of the sun. He looked utterly spent, his shoulders slumped, and there was a week's growth of greying beard on his gaunt features.

'Glad to see you, Hart,' Bland growled, forcing a grin. 'We've been running ourselves ragged over the past month, and ain't done a thing to change the situation. Radd and his gang have vanished into thin air. We've had many reports of his whereabouts, but can't catch up with him.'

'You should have been in Broken Ridge two hours ago,' Hart said grimly, and explained about the bank robbery.

Groans escaped the possemen and Bland cursed emphatically.

'And you're on Radd's trail already,' Bland commented when he had recovered from his shock. He got down stiffly from his saddle and dropped to one knee to examine the tracks. 'Yeah, one of these sets is Radd's hoss all right. I'd know that animal's prints anywhere. We're heading back to town. We've about come to the end of our rope. I'm gonna call off my hunt for Radd now you're back, Hart. I wish you luck. You performed a miracle when you got Radd the first time, and I hope you can repeat it'

'Have you any idea who passed him the pistol when he escaped?' Hart demanded.

Bland shook his head. 'It was done at night. No one saw anyone or anything. I blame myself for not seeing the weakness in having Radd in that particular cell. The window was not large enough for a man to climb through so it was not considered a danger.'

Hart nodded. 'I'll report back to you when I've had a look around,' he said. 'With any luck I'll tote Radd back in irons.'

'Well, good luck. We certainly can't catch him.' Bland turned his horse and departed with the posse strung out behind. Hart watched them heading in the direction of Bleak Ridge.

Hart's face was harshly set when he continued to follow the tracks heading into the south-west. Later, when he halted to rest his horse and was eating cold food, sitting on a rock in a defile, he heard the sound of a horse approaching his position from along his back trail. He sprang up, and his pistol was in his hand when he flattened against a tall rock and craned forward to get a glimpse of the newcomer.

A rider was descending into the defile, and Hart saw a familiar bearded face. The rider was watching the ground, apparently following the tracks that had occupied Hart's attention, and Hart cocked his pistol as he recognized the man as Pete Sewell, another prominent member of Radd's gang. He sprang forward as Sewell came around an outcrop, grasped the reins of the horse, and thrust his muzzle under Sewell's nose.

The horse tried to rear but Hart held it tightly. Sewell half-reached for his holstered gun, then changed his mind, for Hart's muzzle was gaping starkly at him only a foot from his face.

'Howdy, Sewell,' Hart greeted. 'Looks like you and me are riding the same trail. So it was you in Bleak Ridge watching Radd's back. I guess you shot at me, huh? I should have remembered that Radd always covers his back.'

'You should be dead,' Sewell replied, scowling. His dark eyes were narrowed, filled with the glitter of desperation. 'I tried for a head shot, and saw you go down in the dust. I figured you'd cashed your chips, so what are you doin' out here?'

'The same as you. I'm after Radd. Who sprung him loose from the jail in Bleak Ridge?'

'That would be telling.' Sewell grinned. 'You know lightning don't strike twice in the same spot so you shouldn't have any luck this trip. You took Radd unawares the first time but he'll be ready for you now. You never give up, huh?'

'That's right. We'll ride along together. I expect you know where Radd is headed, huh? It would save me a lot of time if you led the way to his hidy-hole. Where is he making for — Mesquite Valley or Blanco Canyon?'

'I don't know. That's why I'm following his tracks.'

'You don't expect me to believe that.' Hart grinned. 'We'll talk about it again later. Step down from that saddle and keep your hand away from your gun.'

Sewell dismounted and raised his hands. Hart disarmed the man, took handcuffs from his saddlebag and snapped them around Sewell's thick wrists.

'Are you hungry?' Hart demanded, and the outlaw shook his head. 'So which way do we ride?' Hart continued.

'You're a better tracker than me,' Sewell countered.

'I don't have to warn you about trying to escape, do I? I never lost a prisoner in ten years of riding with the Rangers, and I'd hate for you to be the first to spoil my record.'

Sewell did not answer. He climbed back into his saddle. Hart took the reins of Sewell's horse and wrapped them around his saddle horn. They continued at a canter, and Hart resumed his study of the tracks.

There were many hard places where the tracks faded, and Hart had to dismount and cast around until he found them again. He made camp in a stand of cottonwoods when the light failed, and full darkness had set in by the time they had eaten. He opened Sewell's handcuffs and passed one cuff around a projecting branch of a fallen tree before snapping it back on Sewell's wrist.

'See you in the morning,' he said as he settled himself in his blankets.

Hart slept easily in the knowledge that his prisoner could not escape, and opened his eyes at first light to see Sewell lying disconsolately anchored to the tree.

'We've got a lot of riding to do today,' Hart remarked as he arose. 'It looks like Radd is making for Mesquite Valley. We'll know for certain later on, and if that is the case then I'll swing south to Maladoro and drop you off in the jail there. How does that sound to you?'

Sewell made no comment and they ate breakfast before moving off. Hart pushed on steadily until around noon, when he was pretty sure the tracks Radd and his bunch were leaving were heading for Mesquite Valley. He continued following the tracks until it was time to cut off to Maladoro, and was riding into the little town by late afternoon.

Tom Anstrom, the deputy sheriff in charge of the law in that part of the county, was a tall, thin man with piercing blue eyes. He was seated behind his desk when Hart ushered his prisoner into the big office. Anstrom was an older man, grizzled, and well versed in the law. His eyes gleamed with recognition when he set eyes on Sewell.

'I know that face,' he said. 'Where did you pick him up?'

Hart explained about the bank robbery in Bleak Ridge.

'I got a feeling Radd has gone into Mesquite Valley,' he added. 'I'll leave Sewell with you while I take a look around out there.'

'Sure thing. Do you want any help? Deputy Sheriff Bill Catton is in town from San Fedora. There's no action out his way, and he'd admire to ride with you. If you're following Radd's gang then you might need some extra guns when you catch up with him.'

'I usually work alone,' Hart replied, 'but I have a hunch that Radd and his gang are in Mesquite Valley right now, so I will need help to take them. Can you round up a dozen good possemen? If we could get the drop on Radd and his bunch we can clean them out. They've been having things their own way far too long, but I got a hunch that Radd is running out of luck.'

'Sure thing.' Anstrom made Sewell empty his pockets on the desk and then locked the outlaw in a cell. 'It'll take me thirty minutes to have a posse ready,' he said. 'If there's anything you need to do around town while you're waiting then now is the time to do it.'

'Sure. I need some supplies, and a meal right now would set me up.'

Hart left the jail and went to the store. He ordered the supplies he needed and then went along to a restaurant, where he paused just long enough to get a decent meal and some coffee. The sun was in the western half of the sky when he went back to the law office, where a group of townsmen were waiting with horses. Bill Catton, the deputy from San Fedora, was eager to ride with Hart.

'I've got to ride over to San Fedora when I've finished with Radd,' Hart told Catton. 'What can you tell me about Sam Straker at Double S?'

'Sam?' Catton frowned. 'I ain't heard that he's got trouble. Truth to tell, I don't reckon anyone would wanta tangle with that old man. He was a Ranger in his youth, and made quite a name for himself along the border. You think he's got trouble?'

'I was ordered to call on him,' Hart replied. 'Sam is old these days, and probably needs help to do a job he could have managed years ago.'

The posse rode out with Hart at their head and headed for Mesquite Valley. They covered fifteen miles before sunset, made camp during the hours of darkness, and were on the move as the sun showed over the horizon next morning. By evening they were nearing the valley, and Hart could still see hoof-prints in the dust, although he was no longer following them for he was aware of the gang's destination.

Mesquite Valley followed the lie of the country in a south-west direction, curving toward the Mexican border. Hart had visited the valley several times in his hunt for Radd and knew the area well. He led the posse away from the faint trail that led into the meandering rift and they rode steadily up an incline that would lead eventually to the rim of the valley.

Hart left his horse and the posse in cover and approached the rim alone and on foot, dropping down to crawl forward over the last yards because he was aware that Radd maintained a strict watch on all approaches to his hideout. When he was able to look down into the valley he saw ten horses in a pole corral off to his right, and, although unable see it, knew there was a cabin in the trees to the left of the corral.

The setting sun glinted on the narrow stream that coursed along the whole length of the valley, and Hart admired the scene as he sat back on his heels and looked around. He decided to wait for pre-dawn darkness before moving in on the hideout, went to unsaddle his horse. Then he informed the posse of his plan for capturing the gang before taking some rest himself.

Hart was awake and moving around when dawn began to relieve the darkness of passing night. A breeze blew into his face as he stood beside his horse and ate cold food. The posse was quiet, and they left their horses in cover when they moved off to perform their grim duty. The sky to the east turned pink and then red. Hart took his Winchester, checked his pistol, and moved slightly to his right to a game trail that led down to the floor of the valley, followed closely by the ten possemen. Moving with the utmost caution, he led the descent of the difficult path, and daylight was apparent by the time they reached level ground.

Hart ordered the possemen to follow him closely in single file and they moved forward briskly. The sun was peering into the valley over the eastern rim by the time they reached the corral, and Hart sent three possemen to circle the cabin under the trees to cut off any escape from the rear. The fact that there were now only five horses standing in the corral did not escape Hart's gaze, and he was disappointed. Half the outlaw gang must have departed in the night.

Intense silence covered the valley. Daylight was strengthening and shadows had diminished. Hart looked around, satisfied himself that the possemen were in position, and led the way towards the cabin.

The door of the cabin was opened while Hart was still a dozen paces from it and a man emerged carrying a bucket. He stepped clear of the cabin before checking his surroundings, and when he saw the approaching possemen he halted, dropped the bucket, and reached for his holstered pistol.

Hart fired his levelled pistol and saw dust fly from the right shoulder of the outlaw's shirt. The man pitched forward on to his face as the crash of the shot hammered through the silence and echoed across the valley. Hart led the possemen forward and charged into the cabin, catching four outlaws in the act of rising from their blankets and reaching for their guns.

Two outlaws managed to draw weapons but were too slow to use them. Shots blasted and the attempted resistance ended abruptly. Both men were hit and fell to the ground, and the remaining two raised their hands in surrender.

Hart was disappointed when he realized that Buck Radd was not in the cabin, and neither was Ike Gotch. When the two unwounded prisoners had been shackled, Hart confronted them.

'So where are Radd and Gotch?' Hart demanded

'Never heard of them,' one of the prisoners replied.

Hart studied the man's face and saw defiance showing in his dark eyes.

'You're Hank Millwood,' he said. 'I recognize you as one of Buck Radd's gang. I saw you with Radd and the gang in the street in Bleak Ridge a few days ago when the bank there was robbed. I got you dead to rights, mister, so open up and tell me what I wanta know.'

'Who the hell are you?' Millwood demanded.

'Mike Hart, Texas Ranger, and I've got a deputy sheriff riding with the posse. So where is Radd? There were ten horses in the corral last night, and now there are only five. I wanta know where Radd and four men were heading when they rode out.'

The prisoners were not disposed to answer questions and Hart left the cabin and went to the corral. He spent some minutes studying the ground and reading the signs that were plain in the dust. Five riders had departed from the valley during the night, and they had travelled fast. He returned to the cabin and sent two possemen up to the rim of the valley to fetch the horses, and then searched through the cabin.

He was disappointed at missing Buck Radd, but the gang boss was at the other end of the tracks he had left when riding out of the valley, and Hart intended following the outlaw even if the trail led into Hell itself.

3

It was almost noon by the time the prisoners were started on their way to the jail in Broken Hill with Bill Catton leading the posse. Hart watched them pull out and, when he was alone, mounted and followed the tracks of the five horses that had headed up the valley. He rode fast, and barely checked the trail because there was only one direction Radd could go. Hart's mind ranged on ahead of his horse in an effort to guess at Radd's likely destination, and he reached the top end of the valley by late afternoon to ride the high ground. Radd's tracks led in a northwesterly direction, and there were few towns of any size along the Mexican border.

Accustomed to travelling alone, Hart camped in a coulee that night, savouring the solitude, his mind engaged in the problem of what Radd was doing and where the outlaw was going. He was linked to the gang boss only by the tracks he was following, and, an expert tracker, he had no doubt that he would eventually recapture his elusive quarry.

Dawn found him following the trail out of the higher reaches of the valley. The tracks of five horses were still plain upon the ground. Hart reined in when he spotted wheel-tracks where a wagon had stopped. He dismounted and studied the ground, his expression hardening when he saw two spent 44.40 Winchester cartridges lying on the ground beside the wheel-marks. The five horses had halted for some time — their hoof-marks showed where they stamped the ground and grazed — and then they had gone on, following their original direction. The wagon had turned around and headed back the way it came.

Hart rode on, studying the ground ahead, and it was not long before he saw the white canvas cover of a prairie schooner moving slowly over the rough ground. He spurred his horse to catch up with the vehicle, and was only yards behind it when the muzzle of a rifle appeared in the opening in the back of the canvas top and fired at him. Hart ducked as a bullet crackled past his head and swung his horse to the left. He rode fast as a second shot blasted, and he felt the tug of a bullet in the tall crown of his Stetson.

A young woman peered at Hart around the canvas from the driving-seat and he saw her lips moving as she shouted at someone in the back of the wagon. She hauled on the reins and stopped the team. Hart approached cautiously, his right hand close to his holstered gun.

'Why did you shoot at me?' he demanded, reining in beside the girl.

A youth of about sixteen years stuck his head into view from behind the girl. The muzzle of a rifle appeared and covered Hart, but the girl pushed the muzzle away.

'He might be another of them, Sis,' the boy said harshly.

'I'm Mike Hart, Texas Ranger. I'm trailing five outlaws, and my guess is that you've tangled with them. I saw where you stopped back there, and spotted two cartridge cases on the ground.'

'I'm Cindy Harmon,' the girl replied. Her face was streaked with tears. She jerked her head towards the youth. 'He's my brother Hal. Five men stopped us. They told us the valley was private, and when my pa grabbed his rifle one of the men shot him. Another shot Ma. We turned around to head back to Cotton-wood Creek.'

'Where are your parents?' Hart enquired.

'In the wagon. They're both dead.'

'Can you describe the men who did the shooting?'

'The one who killed Pa was big, dark-looking, with hard brown eyes and an ugly face. He had a scar that started in his right eyebrow and curved down across his cheek. The man who shot Ma was tall and thin, fair-haired, and he had a long, drooping moustache that reached down his chin. He was laughing when he killed Ma. I thought they were gonna shoot Hal and me, but the man with the scar told me to take the wagon back to Cottonwood Creek.'

'The man with the scar is Buck Radd,' Hart said. 'The other is Ike Gotch, I reckon. They are bankrobbers — killers. I think you're lucky to be alive. Is there anything I can do for you?'

'No, thanks.' The girl shook her head. 'We'll be all right so long as those men don't come back'

'I'm on their trail, and I don't think they'll turn back.' Hart turned his horse away and took up the trail again. He glanced back over his shoulder and saw the wagon on the move once more. A sigh escaped him as he followed the prints of the five robbers. Buck Radd had a lot to answer for.

Passing out of the top end of the

valley, Hart reined in to consider the general direction of the tracks. They were not heading for Cottonwood Creek but seemed to be making for San Fedora, which was very close to the Mexican border. Hart knew the area well and wondered at Radd's intentions.

He continued, and reined in sharply when he topped a rise and spotted a rider coming towards him. He backed his horse off the skyline and waited. Minutes later he heard hoof-beats approaching and drew his pistol. The next instant the rider appeared, and Hart recognized Jake Cullen, a member of Radd's gang.

Cullen reined in quickly at the sight of Hart and his right hand sped to the butt of his holstered pistol.

'Hold it,' Hart rapped. 'Don't make me kill you, Cullen.'

The outlaw froze with his hand on his gun, then raised both hands.

'You're Hart, the Ranger, ain't yuh?' Cullen demanded.

'You got it on the nail. What are you doin' out this-away?'

'Just riding.'

'Where is Radd making for?'

'I ain't seen him in days.'

'I'm following the tracks of five horses. I guess you were one of the five, and Radd has sent you some place else on an errand. I caught up with that wagon in the valley and learned that Radd and Gotch killed a man and a woman. So where are you headed now, and what's on Radd's mind?'

Cullen did not reply. Hart could barely contain his impatience.

'Get rid of your hogleg,' he rapped. 'I'm taking you in, Cullen. I saw you in the street with Radd in Bleak Ridge a few days ago and I'm arresting you for being concerned with the bank robbery there.'

Cullen disarmed himself. Hart rode forward and swung his fist in a vicious hook. His knuckles connected with Cullen's chin and the outlaw uttered a cry as he fell sideways out of his saddle.

Hart dismounted, grasped Cullen, and pulled him up-right.

'I want some straight answers from you, so open up,' he grated harshly. 'Why are you riding back this way?'

'To check our back trail. Radd had a hunch we were being followed.'

'Radd and his hunches!' Hart grimaced. 'They'll get him killed one of these days.'

Hart handcuffed Cullen and thrust the outlaw back into his saddle. He continued, following the tracks patiently, leading Cullen's horse, and they rode through the wilderness for the rest of the day, the hours passing slowly, the nature of the terrain unchanging.

Hart camped in an arroyo that night, and spent the following day trailing the hoof-prints. He found the spot where Cullen had left Radd to check their back trail, and the four sets of tracks continued straight to San Fedora. It was evening when Hart sighted the little border town, and shadows were long across the street when he reined in to look over the adobe buildings. Yellow lamplight was issuing from many windows. He urged his tired horse forward, his keen gaze missing no details of his surroundings as he moved along the street to the sheriff's office.

A guitar was being strummed in a *cantina*, the tune strangely melancholy. San Fedora was more Mexican than North American, although it was on the Yankee side of the border. A man was standing in the open doorway of the law office when Hart reached it. Velvet darkness was closing in on the dusty town. Stars were twinkling in the deep blue of the sky, but, as yet, the breeze had lost none of its heat.

'Howdy, Hart.' A deputy sheriff badge on Frank Burnside's chest twinkled in the lamplight as he stirred. 'Who you got there?'

'Howdy, Frank. This is Jake Cullen, one of Buck Radd's gang. The town seems quiet. I've trailed Radd and some of his boys here all the way from Mesquite Valley.'

'Heck, I ain't seen hide or hair of them around here! Bill Catton is away at the moment.' Burnside was a big man, wide-shouldered and powerful.

'Yeah, I saw Bill in Broken Hill.' Hart dragged Cullen out of his saddle and pushed him towards the door of the office. 'Let's get this bozo behind bars and then I'll tell you what's been going on. I got a feeling Radd and his three men are in town, lying low, and we'd better flush them out before they start doing what they came for.'

'You think Radd is planning to hit the bank?' Burnside moved back into the office and Cullen crossed the threshold, hands above his shoulders. 'Turn out your pockets,' Burnside ordered, and searched Cullen after the outlaw had complied, relieving him of a few scanty belongings.

Hart stood motionless with his pistol levelled at the hip. Cullen was locked in a cell, and Hart holstered his gun.

'I'll take care of my horse and then look around town to see if I can spot

Radd or Gotch,' he said. 'The charge against Cullen is taking part in the bank raid in Bleak Ridge a few days ago. Money was stolen, and a bank teller was shot dead.'

'That's beginning to be a trade mark of the Radd gang,' Burnside observed. 'You want I should go with you looking for them outlaws?'

'No. I'll handle it.' Hart departed and stood in the shadows for some moments, looking around. The breeze was losing some of its heat now, but Hart was sweating and parched. He led his and Cullen's horses as he went along to the bright lights of the saloon that was opposite the brick-built bank, and tethered both animals to a tie rail nearby.

The sound of a guitar being strummed came from inside the saloon, and a female singer was wailing a plaintive Mexican song. Hart paused at the batwings and peered into the saloon. A dozen men were present, some bellied up to the bar and others engaged in gambling at the small tables. Hart pushed through the swing-doors and walked to the bar, badly needing a drink.

He gulped down a tall glass of beer and struggled against the temptation to have another. He had to locate the bank robbers, if they were in town, and he didn't think they would be parading around openly. If they had come to San Fedora to rob the bank they would not want to be seen before opening time the next morning.

He collected the two horses and led them along the street to the livery barn. As he approached the big open doorway of the stable he heard a loud whistle that echoed in the silence. Instantly alert, his right hand dropped down upon his gun butt as he paused by a water-trough to permit the horses to drink. The silence continued, and when he dragged the animals away from the trough he led them into the barn, his senses sharpened.

A lamp was suspended above the doorway, casting deep shadows beyond the small circle of light shining directly on the ground beneath it. Hart took care of the horses without incident, his mind on his surroundings rather than on what he was doing, and he stood for a moment in the shadows of the stall before leaving the stable.

When straw rustled to his right, Hart's pistol leaped into his hand.

'Who's there?' he challenged.

'Señor Hart. I am a friend,' a Mexican voice replied. 'I saw you ride into town. There are *bandidos* in San Fedora. I am Hernando Silvera, and the bad men are in the *cantina* where my sister Carla works. She is afraid of the bad man, Buck Radd, and when she heard you were in town she told me to warn you.'

'News travels fast,' Hart remarked. 'Will you show yourself, Silvera?'

'No, señor. It is too dangerous. There are three men with Radd, and they are talking bad. The town is not safe with such men around.'

'Sure, I understand. Thanks for the

warning. Are you talking about the Mexican *cantina* at the far end of the street?'

'*Sí, señor.*'

'OK. I'll get some help and visit it at once.'

Straw rustled as Silvera departed. Hart holstered his pistol and left the stable to walk back to the law office. Frank Burnside was seated behind the desk, writing a report, and Hart acquainted him with the news. Burnside got to his feet immediately, his right hand dropping to the butt of his holstered gun.

'I know Silvera and his sister,' he said. 'You can rely on them.' He drew his pistol and checked its loads. 'Let's go take Radd,' he said tersely.

'Sure,' Hart agreed.

They left the office and walked along the street to the far end of town. The night was quiet. Stars were strewn thickly across the velvet sky, glinting brightly in the astral gloom. A stiff breeze was blowing across the town, still hot from the long sunlit hours and perfumed by the purple sage. Hart steeled himself for action, wanting Buck Radd dead or alive.

The *cantina* was in dense shadow, and lamplight showed dimly at two small front windows. Hart saw a figure standing outside the door, which turned quickly to enter the low building at their approach.

'Shall we go in together or do you want I should cover the back door?' Burnside asked.

'Stay with me,' Hart decided, and they approached the adobe building with drawn pistols.

A man emerged from the *cantina* while Hart was still several paces from the door and halted in the doorway. His face was shadowed, but Hart could see enough to recognize Ike Gotch, and he was surprised that Gotch was not holding his pistol, certain that the alarm had been raised. He stepped in close and jabbed the muzzle of his gun against the outlaw's side.

'I got you dead to rights, Gotch,' he declared. 'Hands up.'

Gotch raised his hands, speechless in shock. Burnside moved in and disarmed the outlaw. Gotch recovered quickly from his surprise.

'Where in hell did you spring from, Hart?' he demanded, his voice thin. 'If you're looking for Radd you're out of luck. He pulled out ten minutes ago. He had a hunch we were being followed, and ducked out in case someone like you was on his tail. You've been following us for days, huh? Radd had a hunch someone was on our trail.'

'Keep him covered, Frank, while I check out this place,' Hart said. 'Kill him if he tries to escape.'

He thrust Gotch out of the doorway and stalked into the low building, his gun hand resting against his hip, its muzzle pointing downwards . . . There were four Mexicans inside the *cantina*, looking tense, and the big Mexican bartender was sweating profusely. Hart walked to the nearest end of the bar.

'Where's Buck Radd?' he demanded.

'He left by the back door, him and some others,' the bartender replied. 'They are bad men; they threatened us, saying they will come back and shoot us if we talk about them.'

'Where did they go?' Hart demanded. 'Did they have their horses outside?'

'There were horses out back,' the bartender agreed. 'I heard the big man with the scar on his face say to the man who stayed behind that they were riding out to the Double S ranch and would come back to town in the morning.'

Hart frowned. He was planning to visit the Double S when he could get around to it because Captain Buckbee had asked him to call on Sam Straker. The fact that Radd was riding out to the Double S opened up a new aspect on the situation and caused Hart to reconsider his immediate action.

He went back outside to find Burnside covering Gotch.

'Let's put Gotch behind bars,' Hart said, and they went back to the law office.

With the outlaw safely in a cell, Hart questioned Burnside about the local situation.

'Sam Straker owns Double S,' he said. 'Has he got any kind of trouble?'

Burnside frowned. 'What makes you ask about Straker? I don't reckon anyone, not even Radd, could trouble old Sam.'

'I got orders to call on him, which usually means trouble for someone, and the bartender in the *cantina* overheard Radd tell Gotch he was going out to Double S and would be back in town tomorrow morning. I'd like to go out to Double S immediately. Can you get someone to show me the way?'

'I can do better than that.' Burnside grinned. 'Straker's granddaughter, Beth, is in town. She came in from the ranch this afternoon and is staying at the hotel.'

'I'll talk to her.' Hart left the office and walked along the gloomy street, his thoughts deep. What he didn't need at the moment were complications of any kind.

He entered the lobby of the hotel and

addressed the tall, thin woman who was seated at the reception desk.

'Evening, ma'am. I understand there's a Miss Beth Straker staying here, and I'd like to see her.'

'Miss Straker is in the dining-room right this minute,' the woman replied, getting to her feet.

Hart nodded and walked into the dining-room. His gaze was drawn immediately to a young woman in her early twenties who was seated at a corner table. She was dressed in range clothes — faded blue denims, with a small grey Stetson suspended at her back by the chinstrap around her neck. She was in the company of a tall, smooth-looking man, probably in his middle thirties, who was smartly dressed in a brown store suit. His black hair was slicked down, and Hart gained the impression that he was a cardslick. The man's keen brown eyes missed nothing going on around him, and he even looked up and met Hart's gaze across the dining-room.

'That's Miss Straker,' the receptionist said, coming to Hart's side. 'She's sitting with Brent Hallam, the owner of this hotel. I suspect there will be a wedding within the next year. Shall I inform Miss Straker that you wish to talk to her? Or I could give her a message if you wish to see her alone.'

'It looks like she's finished eating,' Hart observed. 'I'll wait in the lobby while you fetch her. My business is kind of urgent.'

'Who shall I say is calling on her?'

'Mike Hart. She might know me by name but I wouldn't stake my life on it.'

Hart went back into the lobby and waited by the desk. A moment later the receptionist reappeared followed by Beth Straker. The girl was attractive, Hart was aware, with blond hair framing a pretty face that had blue eyes and a pert mouth. But Hart noted that her eyes were filled with worry, and she seemed ill at ease.

'Sorry to drag you away from your table, Miss Straker,' Hart said smoothly.

'What's wrong?' she asked. 'Has something happened to my grand-father?'

'I think we'd better sit down and talk. I'm Mike Hart, Texas Ranger, and I'm under orders to call at Double S to see Sam Straker.' He took hold of Beth's arm and led her to a small table while he explained recent events. By the time he got around to mentioning Buck Radd and the outlaws the girl's worry had turned to anger.

'I don't know what kind of a hold Radd has on Grandfather, but that outlaw comes and goes at the ranch like he owns the place. Grandfather won't talk to the law, but I eventually got him to contact Captain Buckbee of the Rangers.'

'The Cap'n has been a mite busy of late, but he's sent me to talk to your grandfather. I've had trouble with Radd, but got the word that he would be at Double S tonight. I reckoned to get some background information from you before riding out to the spread. Is

Radd is a regular visitor to Double S?'

'I've seen him around there a few times. I've asked Grandfather why he doesn't set the crew on Radd, and I'm surprised he doesn't do that, seeing that he was a Texas Ranger in his youth and is always talking about his exploits along the border. If I didn't know better, I would say Radd has some kind of a hold on Grandfather, but that seems ridiculous.'

'It sure sounds like it,' Hart agreed. 'I'm gonna ride out to the ranch, and need someone to guide me. Are you staying in town tonight?'

'I had planned to, but I won't if you're going out to Double S. I came into town to sort out some personal business, but that can wait. I'll ride with you, and I hope you'll catch Radd at the ranch. It's about time he was put behind bars, where he belongs.'

'Can you throw any light at all on why your grandfather tolerates Radd out at the ranch?'

Beth shook her head. 'I haven't

learned a thing, and I've been watching and listening. Grandfather is close-lipped about Radd. I've warned him that he could be in bad trouble if the law found out about Radd's comings and goings but he doesn't seem to care about the consequences of his actions.'

'I'd like to hit the trail soon as I can.' Hart said, frowning. 'How far is it to Double S?'

'Fifteen miles.'

'Is there any kind of trouble on this range?'

'None that I know of.' Beth shook her head. 'There's the odd case of cattle-stealing, but it isn't large-scale. Apart from Radd's robberies, the county is pretty much tamed. But I'm badly worried about Grandfather. I'll get my horse and meet you in front of the law office in, say, fifteen minutes.'

'Thanks. I'm real sorry to drag you away from your companion. I hope he'll understand.'

'He's Brent Hallam, and owns the saloon, among other things. He's very understanding. He's offered to buy Double S because Grandfather is getting too old to run the spread. I thought it was a good idea, because Brent said we could still live out there, but when I broached it to Grandfather he wouldn't hear of it, and banned Brent from coming out to the ranch.'

'I guess a man like your grandfather would be real touchy about a matter like that.' Hart got to his feet. 'I'll fetch my horse.'

He departed. He paused in the shadows outside the saloon and looked around the street, his eyes filled with calculation as he considered what he had learned, which was that Sam Straker was in trouble and Buck Radd was somehow implicated.

He started along the street towards the law office, his thoughts ranging over the situation, and the face of Brent Hallam seemed to be a sticking point in his mind. The hotelier came across as a bad man, and Hart made a mental note to check on him later. He was passing the front of the saloon when a thin ribbon of orange flame stabbed at him from across the street. Hart went down instantly, and his gun was in his hand as the sound of a shot blasted out the brooding silence.

4

A slug smacked into the front of the saloon just above Hart's head and his teeth glinted in a defiant grin as he returned fire, the big .45 pistol bucking in his hand. Gunsmoke drifted around his head. The gun across the street shut down and Hart held his fire, listening to the fading echoes grumbling away across the town. His eyes were narrowed, his thoughts fast-moving. Who was out to get him? He knew that every two-bit crook in Texas would take any opportunity to kill him, and, no doubt, his presence in town had been noted by a number of local bad men.

He pushed himself to one knee, gun ready, but there was no reaction from the shadows across the street. He stood up and faded into the dense shadows, listening intently, catching the sound of someone blundering away down an

73

alley. A dog was barking somewhere across town, the insistent sound echoing thinly in the surrounding heavy silence. He drew a deep breath, restrained it for long moments, and felt his heart pounding. The sound of hurried footsteps along the street warned him that someone was coming to investigate the shooting.

'Hold it right there,' he challenged when a tall figure emerged from the shadows.

'Burnside,' came the brittle answer. 'That you, Hart?'

'Yeah. Someone took a pot-shot at me from across the street. He's gone now, and I think I might have caught him with a slug.'

'I'll take a look around.' Burnside stepped off the sidewalk to cross the street.

'Before you go,' Hart said. 'I'm riding out shortly, heading for Double S, and Beth Straker is going with me. I'll be back in town tomorrow before the bank opens, in case Radd has ideas in that direction, but I'm hoping to run across him out at the ranch. Something is going on out there, and the sooner I check it out the better. Beth Straker seems quite concerned about her grandfather and I ain't surprised, seeing that the oldster is allowing Radd to come and go as he pleases.'

'OK. Watch your step.'

'There's one thing you can fill me in on,' Hart said as Burnside moved away, The big deputy paused. 'Brent Hallam. What can you tell me about him?'

'Hallam!' Burnside turned to confront Hart. 'What's your interest in him?'

'Just a gut feeling. There's something about him that triggers an alarm in my mind.'

'I know what you mean.' Burnside nodded. 'I've felt like that about him from the first moment I saw him, and I still can't put a finger on what makes me restless in his company. I've checked him out and he comes up clean, although he worked as a gambler for some years before he came here to take over the hotel, which was left to him by his pa, Henry Hallam. I must say that Brent seems to be a reformed character. I ain't seen him touch a deck of cards in the three years he's been around. The only thing I got against him is the two bouncers he employs. They are a couple of real hardcases, and he doesn't really need them in the hotel business.'

'Thanks, Frank.' Hart nodded. 'We'll talk some more when I get back tomorrow. I've got to be riding now.'

'So long.' Burnside vanished into the darkness across the street. Hart turned and made his way to the stable, wondering whether Hallam or one of his men had shot at him.

Beth Straker appeared in the doorway of the hotel as Hart passed it, and they walked to the livery barn together.

'I heard the shooting and guessed you were involved in it,' Beth observed. 'Is that right?'

'Yeah. I'm always getting shot at,'

Hart replied. 'It goes with the job, but, in case you're wondering, I never get used to dodging lead.'

They saddled up and rode out of town and, on the trip to Double S Hart questioned Beth closely but failed to gain any real information on the situation existing at the ranch. The girl was plainly reticent when Hart tried to talk about Brent Hallam, and he wondered how interested she was in the hotelier.

It was well past midnight when Beth reined up on a knoll.

'Double S is just the other side of the ridge in front of us,' she explained. 'We'd better not ride straight in just in case Radd and his men are there.'

'I couldn't ride in without causing trouble, if Radd is there,' Hart agreed, 'but you can, huh?'

'Sure. They wouldn't think anything of my coming and going.'

'So go ahead and find out what you can about Radd's plans, if he's there. I'll show up at the back door of the house in, say, an hour, and you come out and talk to me. How does that sound?'

'Fine.' Beth shook her reins and went on.

Hart sat his mount, listening to her departure. When silence returned he dismounted and walked forward, striking rising ground and ascending to the crest. From the top of the ridge he saw lights in the middle distance, and trailed his reins and hunkered down to wait out the time.

Thinking over the situation, Hart wondered what kind of trouble had hit Sam Straker. The Double S rancher was an ex-Ranger who came from a breed of men who were well able to take care of themselves. So why was Radd getting entangled with the likes of Straker? The outlaw boss was experienced enough to know that what he was doing was wrong; so what was the attraction?

The flow of questions through Hart's mind was interminable, and no satisfactory answers presented themselves.

When he arose to continue to the ranch he was little the wiser about what was going on.

He angled for the rear of the ranch house, moving at a walk in order to remain soundless. He dismounted fifty yards out from the rear of the house, tethered his horse in cover, and walked in the rest of the way to position himself in dense shadows just a few feet from the back door. The rear of the house was in darkness; the surrounding silence heavy and ominous.

Starshine gave Hart sufficient light to observe his surroundings and he stood with a cooling breeze in his face. He blinked tiredly but his caution was at its top level, and his right hand was close to the butt of his holstered pistol. He waited stolidly, and did not move when the sound of bolts being withdrawn on the inside of the kitchen door reached his ears.

The door was opened slowly and Hart flexed the fingers of his right hand. A woman's figure appeared in the doorway and he stepped forward quickly. Beth gasped at his sudden appearance.

'Come in.' she invited. 'It's quite safe. Radd was here with a couple of his men but left almost immediately, and Grandpa went with him.'

'Your grandfather left the ranch?' Hart frowned. 'Of his own free will?'

'It seems so. Joe Clack, our cook, was in the house when Radd turned up, and he said Pa didn't argue with Radd when he was invited to ride out. He saddled up and left, telling Joe he would be back tomorrow. I don't know what to make of it, the way Grandpa gives in to Radd.'

'It doesn't make sense,' Hart agreed. 'Your grandfather is an ex-Ranger, and wouldn't willingly have anything to do with a known outlaw. So what's going on here? Sam Straker contacted Captain Buckbee and asked to see a Ranger, and a man doesn't do that unless he's got some trouble he can't handle himself. Can you tell me anything about your grandfather's business?'

'He's never mentioned any trouble, and I would have noticed if things were going wrong. But there is nothing amiss. Life has been quite trouble-free.'

'Why is Buck Radd hanging around here? Has he visited the ranch many times?'

'Several times over the past month, and I didn't learn that he is an outlaw until a few days ago.'

'And your grandfather hasn't seemed worried or concerned about anything?'

Beth shook her head. 'Sam is a quiet man, and you'd never know by his expression what he was thinking. I asked him about Radd and all he said was that Radd was someone he knew years ago.'

'Well, there's nothing I can do until daylight,' Hart mused. 'In the morning I'll look for tracks, if your grandfather hasn't returned by then.'

'Come in and I'll get supper for you,' Beth invited.

'Thanks. I'll take you up on that, but

I'd better see to my horse before I think of myself. I'll put Blackie in your barn.'

'I'll show you the way.' Beth picked up a lantern and they left the kitchen.

Hart fetched his horse and rejoined the girl. They walked across to the barn, and Hart drew his pistol quickly when a figure detached itself from the dense shadows surrounding the building and confronted them, lamplight glinting on a rifle he was holding.

'It's OK, Rafe.' Beth said. 'This is a Texas Ranger. He's on the trail of Buck Radd.'

'You've just missed that polecat, Ranger,' Rafe Lambert replied 'I told Sam he was asking for trouble, letting Radd come and go, but Sam ain't a man keen on taking advice, and I reckon he's in a lot of trouble right now, riding off in Radd's company. I don't like it, Beth. You can't trust a skunk like Radd. He's bad medicine, and then some.'

'I agree with you, but there's nothing we can do about the situation until tomorrow.' Beth set down the lantern on a barrel head and watched Hart take care of his horse.

'I'll sleep here in the barn,' Hart decided. 'I want to be up at first light and on my way by the time the sun shows. I'll check out tracks and take out on your grandfather's trail, because I'd sure like to know why he accompanied Radd.'

Rafe Lambert escorted Beth back to the house. Hart settled down on a pile of hay with his provisions and ate cold food before dousing the lamp. He slept until the grey light of dawn peered in through the open doorway of the barn, and was ready saddled to travel by the time the first rays of the sun shone above the eastern horizon.

The ranch yard bore the tracks of many hoofs, and Hart walked around studying them until he had read their significance. He picked out four sets of recent hoof-prints and followed them to the gate, noting that they had headed off in a south-west direction. When he went to the barn for his horse he saw Beth Straker emerging from the house and crossed to her side. The girl was plainly worried and it showed in her eyes.

'I've found tracks,' he told her. 'They're heading into the south-west. I'll see where they lead to, and come back this way to let you know what I find.'

'I'm so worried by Grandfather's actions,' Beth replied. 'It just isn't like him to go off this way.'

'Give me a little time and I'll get down to the hard facts,' Hart replied, as he departed.

He rode steadily in the bright morning sunlight. The tracks led him back to San Fedora, and he reined up and gazed at the stark outlines of the little town. His face was set in an expressionless mask when he went on, and he was braced for bad news when he stepped down from his horse in front of the law office.

Frank Burnside was seated at his desk in the dusty office, and looked up quickly when Hart entered.

'No,' he replied to Hart's question. 'There's been no trouble around here since you left last night. I checked out the alley this morning where you were shot at and found bloodstains in the dust. I followed them until they stopped on the other side of the street. It looked like the man who was hit was making for the hotel. I haven't done anything about that. I was waiting for you to get back, and it might pay us to check on Hallam and his two hardcases. How'd you find matters out at Double S?'

Hart explained and Burnside's expression changed.

'Heck, that doesn't sound like Sam Straker, not by a long rope,' he declared. 'We'd better get on and locate him, huh?'

'I left the tracks on the edge of town to come and talk to you,' Hart said. 'I reckon we better follow them to their end. We'll leave Hallam and his side-kicks until I've got more time. They'll keep.'

They left the office and walked to the end of the street. Hart pointed out the tracks, which angled to the left and made for the back lots on that side of the street. They followed cautiously.

'Looks like they rode into that barn over there,' Burnside commented, peering down at the tracks. 'We reckoned Radd was gonna hit the bank here in town when it opened this morning, but that ain't happened or I'd have heard shooting. So what's going on?'

'Let's look in the barn before I try to answer that question,' Hart responded. His right hand was on the butt of his pistol as they moved in on the building.

The tracks led right into the barn, and Hart drew his pistol. The barn door was closed and a seemingly ominous silence enveloped the place. Hart put a finger to his lips, cautioning silence, and made a circuit of the barn, followed closely by Burnside, until he reached the rear. His keen gaze picked out recent tracks made by three horses leaving the barn and heading out to the range in a north-east direction.

'Four riders rode in and three rode out,' Hart observed.

'So one of them is still inside.' Burnside cocked his drawn pistol.

'Sam Straker, I expect.' Hart's voice was impassive but there was tension in his breast as he reached out with his left hand and eased open the rear door of the barn.

He entered into the dim interior of the low building and moved to one side, pausing until his sight became accustomed to the gloom. A big grey horse was tethered to a manger on the right, champing on a forkful of hay that had been dumped in the manger. The animal raised its head when it sensed Hart's presence, whickered a greeting, and then resumed eating. Hart went forward rapidly; he had spotted the figure of a man lying nearby, hogtied and helpless, but evidently alive.

'It's Sam Straker,' Burnside said, coming to Hart's side.

Hart holstered his pistol and dropped

to one knee beside the bound man. He removed a neckerchief that had been pushed into Straker's mouth and then untied the rawhide used to bind the rancher's hands behind his back. Burnside grasped Straker by an arm and helped him to his feet. Straker was angry and it showed in his livid expression. He shook off Burnside's helping hand, muttering under his breath, and glared defiantly at Hart.

'What happened to you, Sam?' Burnside demanded.

Sam Straker was tall and spare, his back and shoulders ramrod-straight. His craggy face showed age — the middle fifties — and his strikingly blue eyes were filled with bad humour as he gazed at his rescuers. He was dressed in a brown store-suit, and his Stetson was pushed back on his head, revealing a mass of iron-grey hair. He flexed his fingers as if he had been tied too tightly while his keen gaze swung from Burnside to Hart, who lifted aside the lapel of his vest to reveal his Ranger law badge — a small star set in a silver circle — which was pinned to his shirt. Sight of the badge took the edge off Straker's ire.

'I'm Mike Hart, from Amarillo,' Hart said.

'Ed Buckbee sent you, huh?' Straker nodded. 'I wrote to Ed more than four weeks ago. What took you so long getting here, son? We did things differently in my days as a Ranger.'

'I doubt that you did.' Hart smiled. 'Howsomever, I'm here now, and my time was taken up by Buck Radd. I've been trailing him over half of Texas while he's been hiding out on your spread.'

'Now that ain't exactly true.' Straker looked around, saw a crate by the manger, and crossed to it to sit down heavily. He looked up at Hart, his face expressionless, his blue eyes over-bright.

'I'd admire to hear your story,' Hart told him, 'but we were expecting Radd to hit the bank here in town this morning and I need to check that out before I get down to brass tacks with you. I suggest you go along to the jail with Frank and stay there until I can get back to you.'

'Are you arresting me?' Straker's jaw was thrust out pugnaciously. 'Don't judge a pretty woman by her face, son. Appearances can be so wrong.'

'No.' Hart smiled as he shook his head. 'You're not under arrest. I just want to make sure I'll know where to come when I can get around to talking to you some more.'

Straker shrugged and got to his feet. 'OK. I'll go with Burnside, but you can take it from me that Radd ain't gonna hit the bank in town this morning.'

'So you know his plans, huh?' Hart suggested.

Straker shook his head. 'No one knows what Buck Radd is gonna do. I don't believe he even knows himself. I just know some of the things he ain't gonna do, and robbing the bank today is one of them. Take my word on that and you'll save some time and effort.'

'Why did Radd bring you from Double S and leave you hogtied in here?' Hart's voice was soft. He was prepared to give Straker the benefit of the doubt because of his great past, but circumstances seemed stacked against the rancher and only a reasonable explanation could remove the doubts lingering in Hart's mind.

'It was Beth or me.' Straker scowled. 'I finally had a showdown with Radd — told him to stay away from the ranch. He threatened to grab and hold Beth, and I didn't want her suffering in his hands so I offered to ride with him as far as town, and he left me tied in here to gain time getting clear. Radd is a great one for hunches, and he couldn't shake off the feeling that he was being trailed. He wasn't far wrong, huh?'

'Go along to the law office and wait there for me,' Hart directed. 'I need to check out Radd's tracks.'

Hart left the barn and studied the

ground outside. He checked the three sets of tracks that led off into the north-east until he was satisfied that Radd was not circling to enter San Fedora from another direction. He paused on a knoll and looked around. Straker and Burnside were walking away from the barn, and he remained motionless until they disappeared into an alley. When he returned his attention to the three sets of tracks he dropped to one knee and examined them more closely, nodding his head slowly as he decided that one of the horses had not carried a rider when it left. He grinned. Radd was smart. He had left one of his men behind in town and had almost gotten away with it.

With his hand close to his gun butt, Hart went along the nearest alley to the street and walked to the law office. Burnside and Straker were entering the office and Hart looked around the street from force of habit before hurrying to reach them. Burnside frowned when Hart appeared, and Hart acquainted the deputy with the result of his checking.

'Radd is craftier than a wagonload of monkeys,' Burnside observed, shaking his head.

'So who was riding with Radd?' Hart asked Straker.

The rancher sighed and shook his head. 'Radd was breaking in a couple of men new to the gang,' he replied. 'I hadn't seen either of them before. All I know about them is that one was called Hank Wilmer and the other Chuck Denton.'

'Would you know either again if you saw them?' Hart enquired

'Sure. We'll go around town and I'll finger whoever Radd left behind.'

'Now you're being real helpful,' Burnside said with a trace of sarcasm. 'I'll come with you. Let's get moving. Radd has left a man behind to watch the bank, I guess, and we need to put him behind bars pronto.'

Hart nodded and led the way out of the office. He looked around the street when he heard the sound of approaching hoofs, and saw three riders coming towards the office. Surprise filled him when he noted that the foremost was Bull Santee, the bullying deputy from Bleak Ridge. His two companions were hard-bitten men with the mien of long riders — eyes watching their surroundings alertly and hands close to the butts of their holstered guns.

Santee reined up at the edge of the sidewalk and sat his buckskin, eyes glinting as he gazed at Hart with a half-grin on his fleshy face. His expression reminded Hart of a puma about to pounce on its prey.

'What in hell are you doing here?' Burnside demanded when he emerged from the office behind Straker. He glared at Santee in disbelief.

'Sheriff Bland sent me over to help in the hunt for Buck Radd.' Santee grinned. 'I got orders to work with you, Hart, and Ben Gatting and Cal Wenn came with me to help out.'

'I don't need you or anyone else dogging my movements,' Hart replied, eyeing Santee and his two sidekicks with distaste. 'Ride back to Bleak Ridge and tell Bland just that. I'd rather work blindfold than take you on.'

'And I sure as hell don't want you in San Fedora,' Burnside rapped. 'The last time you showed up here; you caused a load of trouble. Turn your horse around and get out of town, Santee. It's lucky Bill Catton is away or he'd have drawn on you.'

'I got my orders from the sheriff.' Santee bristled and his tone turned ragged 'He's the top law man in this county so I'll stay right here until I learn otherwise from him. Go ahead — wire Bland and tell him how you feel about me, and if he says I should pull out then I'll go, but until I get the word from him I'll be camping in the saloon, biding my time.'

Hart watched Santee with narrowed eyes as the big deputy turned his horse and sent the animal along the street at a canter, followed by his two tough companions. The trio rode along to the livery barn at the far end of the street, dismounted to water their horses at the trough in front of the big double doorway, and then disappeared inside the barn.

'I'll get a wire off to Sheriff Bland,' Burnside said. 'I want Santee out of town before he gets set. He's nothing but trouble, and the sheriff must be loco to send him here.'

'I didn't like the look of those two galoots with Santee,' Straker said heavily. 'They're a couple of no-goods, unless I miss my guess. Radd let slip last night that he's ain't worried about the local law, and I reckoned he's got someone on the inside somewhere, working for him. In my estimation, Santee fills that bill just right, and if you give him an inch anywhere along the line, Hart, you could make the biggest mistake of your life.'

'Thanks for the advice, but I got Santee pegged right. I'll talk to him after I've picked up the man Radd has left in town.'

'Let's get to it then,' Burnside said

grimly. 'We run a clean town here, and I'm gonna keep it that way while I'm handling things. Sam, tell me about those two men with Radd. We need to know something about the one we're looking for.'

'I'll know him if I see him,' Straker said. 'I've been pretending to go along with Radd while I waited for a Ranger to show up in response to the letter I sent Ed Buckbee. Now you're here, Hart, I'll do all I can to help you nail Radd. I've kept him on a long rope, and now you can haul him in.'

'Why did Radd look you up, and how come you let him get a hold on you?' Hart asked as they walked along the street.

'I guess Buckbee doesn't know that Radd is Buck Radcliffe, a one-time Ranger who left the service to start his own cattle ranch. But he hit hard times, and was almost wiped out by rustlers, so he took to the self-same trail, stealing cattle before graduating to robbery and murder.'

'Why didn't you give Cap'n Buckbee that information?' Hart demanded. He studied the rancher's craggy face, wondering what was in the man's mind.

'Radd saved my life more than once when we rode together as Rangers.' Straker shook his head. 'Because of that I owed him a couple of favours, but he knows that's over with now. If he shows up around Double S again I'll draw on him.'

Hart, glancing at the rancher, saw determination in Straker's gaze, and nodded, having learned more about Buck Radd in the last five minutes than he had ever known, and a strand of impatience unwound in his mind as he considered the situation. He was certain Straker was not telling him everything, and he couldn't wait to arrest Radd again to get at the truth.

'Let's check out the saloons first,' Burnside suggested.

Hart nodded. They approached the nearest saloon, and were still twenty yards from the batwings when Hart saw a man peer out over the slatted doors. One of the batwings was pushed open slightly and a pistol blasted raucously through the gap, the sound tearing through the silence and sending echoes racing across the town.

5

Hart moved instinctively as he called a warning. He grasped Straker's shoulder and dragged the rancher down on the sidewalk while drawing his pistol. Burnside was also moving, hurling himself sideways against a shop-front before dropping to one knee. The man in the saloon fired again. Hart heard the thud of a slug ripping into the wooden sidewalk and saw splinters fly. He rolled sideways and dropped into the dust of the street, angling the long barrel of his weapon upwards to get a shot at the ambusher.

The gun in the doorway of the saloon fired again and Hart saw Straker jump under the impact of a driving slug. He triggered his Colt and sent three shots through the batwing door about waist-high. Burnside cut loose at the same time, and splinters flew from the thin door. Gun smoke flared, almost obscuring Hart's vision.

Hart thrust himself up from the ground and lunged forward across the sidewalk, shoulders hunched and his gun hand steady. He hit the batwings hard and fast, pushing through them, and went down on the threshold, sliding several feet while his gaze searched for the gunman. He came to rest with his head almost touching a body sprawled on the sanded floor of the saloon, and brought his gun to bear, covering the figure. Gun echoes faded slowly.

Several men were present in the saloon — three standing at the bar and four seated around a gamingtable in a far corner. A bartender was standing behind the long bar, a glass in one hand and a cloth in the other, all movement suspended.; his mouth was agape and shock stained his craggy features.

Hart pushed himself to one knee and looked down at the motionless man, who had blood on his shirt-front but was still breathing. He got to his feet and kicked the man's discarded pistol away before covering the saloon. Sweat was running down his face and he cuffed it away. His ears were ringing from the sound of the quick gun blasts and he swallowed to clear them. There was no movement in the saloon. Hart stepped sideways to the front corner of the bar.

'OK,' he grated. 'Someone tell me what happened in here.'

'That feller was waiting for someone to show up,' the 'tender said. 'He was standing about where you are now, and kept looking out at the street. He's a stranger in town. I never saw him before. Mebbe he was waiting for you to show up.'

'You could be right,' Hart acknowledged.

Hart went to the batwings and looked outside. Burnside was on his knees beside the prostrate Sam Straker; there was blood on the rancher's shirt-front.

'How is he?' Hart called.

'Pretty bad.' Burnside looked up, and then got to his feet. 'I've stopped the bleeding. I'd better hustle for Doc Crane. Did we get the gunnie?'

'Yeah. He's down in here. He must be the man Radd left behind in town. He was shooting at Straker. But I'm wondering why they didn't kill Straker when they had the chance earlier.'

'Before Radd rode out of town, you mean.' Burnside nodded. 'I'll leave the fancy thinking to you, Hart. I'll fetch the doc.'

Hart surveyed the street and saw Santee and his two sidekicks coming along the sidewalk from the livery barn. Townsfolk were appearing on the street, attracted by the shooting. Hart went to Straker's side and dropped to one knee beside the rancher. Straker was unconscious and breathing heavily, his face ashen. There was nothing Hart could do for the ex-Ranger and he straightened as the first of the townsmen arrived. It was Brent Hallam, and the hotelier gazed impassively at Straker.

'Is he alive?' Hallam demanded.

'Just about.' Hart nodded. 'But he's a tough old man, and mebbe the doc will be able to pull him through.'

'Is Beth in town?' Hallam glanced around, his snakelike eyes missing nothing of his surroundings. There was an air of detachment about him that Hart found disconcerting. Hallam seemed to be a man without an ounce of emotion in his make-up.

'No.' Hart shook his head. 'I left her at the Double S last night.'

'Then I'd better ride out there and tell her about this. Who shot him?'

'There's a man lying dead in the saloon — a stranger in town.'

Hallam nodded. His gaze fell upon Santee, and his impassive expression broke for a moment, showing anger which was quickly covered up.

'What's that no-good deputy doing in town?' he demanded.

'It seems no one has a good word for Santee.' Hart was watching the deputy's approach.

'He caused a lot of trouble around here the last time he was in San Fedora,' Hallam said, 'and if he insults Beth again I'll gut-shoot him.'

'Anything I can do?' Santee called, pausing as he reached the batwings of the saloon. There was a fixed grin on his thick lips and his eyes were gleaming. He looked like the cat that had got the cream, and Hart wondered at his attitude.

'The best thing you can do is return to Bleak Ridge,' Hart replied.

'And I better not catch you looking in Beth Straker's direction either!' Hallam rapped.

Santee grinned and swaggered through the batwings into the saloon, followed by his two companions. Hart gazed at the swinging doors for a moment before looking around the street. He saw Frank Burnside emerging from a house followed by a short, fleshy man who was carrying a brown leather bag. The two men came hurrying along the sidewalk.

Doc Crane nodded at Hart when he

arrived, and dropped to his knees beside Sam Straker. He got up again almost immediately and turned to Burnside, his blue eyes narrowed.

'Have him brought to my office, Frank,' Crane said. 'I can't do anything here. And take it easy with him. He looks to be in a bad way. You'd better get word to Beth about this. She should be here.'

'I'll ride out to the ranch and fetch her.' Hallam departed swiftly.

Burnside detailed four men to lift Straker, and Hart followed as the unconscious rancher was carried along the street. He was placed on a table in the doctor's office. The four bearers left, leaving Hart and Burnside with Crane.

'I'll go check up around town,' Burnside said. 'Someone had better keep an eye on Santee. There'll be trouble the minute he gets drunk.'

'I'll be along as soon as I learn of Straker's condition,' Hart said.

Burnside departed and Hart sat

down on a chair in a corner, his mind busy on the situation as he idly watched the doctor's deft movements in treating the unconscious rancher. Silence weighed heavily upon them for many minutes, and then Crane looked up.

'All we can do now is pray,' he said. 'But I think he's got a good chance of pulling through, barring complications.'

Hart nodded and got to his feet. He went out to the street and stood for a moment on the sidewalk, looking around, puzzled by the shooting of Sam Straker. If the dead man in the saloon had been left behind by Radd when he rode out, then why had Radd not killed the rancher during the night? Why had Straker been left hogtied in the barn and then shot publicly? It didn't make sense, unless Radd wanted to be miles away when the murder was committed.

Frank Burnside was standing in a knot of townsmen in front of the saloon and Hart went to join them. He skirted the group and entered the saloon. Santee and his two sidekicks were bellied up to the bar. The dead man had been removed, and a liberal sprinkling of sawdust covered the bloodstains on the floorboards. The 'tender moved along the bar to confront Hart, wiping the bar-top with a damp cloth. He was plainly nervous, but whether he was upset by the shooting or by Santee's presence Hart could only guess.

'Beer,' Hart said, and realized that he was hungry as well as thirsty. 'Can you rustle me up some grub?'

'Sure. What would you like?'

'Anything that's going.' Hart waited until a glass of beer came sliding in front of him, picked it up, and went to a small table situated near the door that led into the rear quarters of the saloon.

The 'tender went through to the kitchen, returning some minutes later. He paused beside Hart.

'Grub will be ready in about twenty minutes,' he reported, and went back behind the bar.

Hart relaxed, and by the time his meal arrived he had decided upon his next move. He had to get on Radd's trail. There was nothing he could do around town while Sam Straker was unconscious. He ate without really taking heed of what was on his plate, and wiped it clean before getting to his feet. He crossed to the bar for another beer, paid the 'tender for the meal, and departed without so much as a glance in Santee's direction.

He went along to the law office. Frank Burnside got to his feet at his desk, a pen in his right hand.

'Just writing a report on the shooting,' he said. 'I can't believe Radd is behind it after leaving Straker hogtied in that barn. What do you make of it?'

Hart shook his head. 'It sure beats me. What you need to do is identify the man we shot. If he is one of Radd's gang then we'll have to wait until Straker is able to identify him. In the meantime, I'm gonna follow Radd's tracks from that barn on the back lot and see where he's heading. I'll be back later.'

'I'd feel a lot happier if Santee and those two tough galoots weren't in town,' Burnside mused. 'I think I can handle Santee if he starts anything, but those two with him change the picture, and then some.'

'I've got the feeling that I'll have to tangle with Santee before this is done,' Hart said grimly, 'but now ain't the right time. I guess you'll just have to keep an eye on him and be ready to move before he does, if he's up to anything bad.'

'Yeah, I guess it's the only way, but it's the hell of a thing when you have to watch a law man for trouble. I sure wish Bill Catton was back. Now, about identifying the guy who shot Sam Straker. We've got Ike Gotch behind bars. Perhaps he'd put a name to the dead man?'

'It's worth a try.' Hart nodded. 'Fetch Gotch out of his cell and we'll pay a visit to the undertaker's parlour.'

Ike Gotch was in a sullen mood when his cell door was unlocked. He emerged like a wolf escaping from a trap, suspicious and wary.

'What was that shooting I heard?' he demanded. 'Have you nailed Radd?'

'Not yet. Radd pulled out with one man and leading the horse of a third man who stayed in town,' Hart explained. 'We suspect that the man who remained behind shot Sam Straker. He's dead and Sam is bad hurt. We want you to look at the dead man and put a name to him, if you can.'

'Why should I help you?' Gotch demanded.

'It's not so much helping us as ensuring that the dead man is buried with his name on a marker. He must have a family somewhere, and they have the right to know what has happened to him.'

'OK, let's take a look at him,' Gotch replied reluctantly.

They went to the undertaker's parlour, where Gotch took one look at the dead man, then turned away.

'That's Dev Eke,' he said. 'He rode

with us for about a year. Now why did he wanta kill Sam Straker?'

'That's a question I need to know the answer to,' Hart responded.

'Well, don't look at me.' Gotch grinned crookedly. 'You got to find the reason without my help.'

They returned Gotch to the jail and Hart prepared to ride out. He walked to the door of the office and gazed around at the street. When he saw the prints made by Santee's horse when the deputy arrived in town, he crossed the sidewalk and bent to study the marks in the thick dust. He had made a study of hundreds of hoof-prints over the years, and retained some in his mind that he could recognize any-where. He noticed a tiny cut in the left front print of the set, where the blacksmith had nicked the metal in the smoothing process.

Burnside was grinning when Hart straightened.

'It might pay you to back-track Santee and find out what he was up to before he arrived here,' Burnside said. 'I've never trusted that guy, and he seems to have got worse over the past year or so.'

'You're right.' Hart nodded. 'I'll bear it in mind until Radd is behind bars again. It's time something was done about Santee.'

Hart mounted his horse and rode to the rear of the barn on the back lot It was a simple job to pick out Radd's tracks with the two attendant sets, and he started away from the barn, aware that he was several hours behind the outlaw gang-leader, although, judging by the prints, Radd was in no hurry to get to where he was going.

Pushing the horse into a canter, Hart moved away from San Fedora, his gaze on the three sets of tracks. He judged that Radd was moving into the north-east, and cast his mind ahead in an effort to pin-point the outlaw's destination. But he did not make a habit of ranging so far ahead mentally, preferring just to follow until he was close enough to his quarry to take direct action.

It was late afternoon when Hart found a spot where one of the riders he was tracking had cut away on his own. After studying the ground he saw that Buck Radd's mount was heading alone towards the little border town of Cottonwood Creek The tracks of the other two horses swung away north.

When darkness came Radd was close enough to Cottonwood Creek to accept that it was Radd's destination. When the tracks were no longer visible he rode on to the town, spotting its yellow lights long before he arrived on the outskirts. He was tired beyond belief, and heaved a long sigh when he reached the livery barn.

He took care of his horse and then made his way to the law office. He knew the town well, as he knew most of the communities in this area, and entered the office to find Lew Walker, the town marshal, drowsing at his desk.

Walker was a tall, heavily built man

whose keen blue eyes showed a wealth of experience. He was about forty years old. and had been in the law-dealing business for more than twenty years.

'Am I glad to see you?' Walker declared at the sight of his visitor. 'I got some real trouble on my hands, and no one to turn to for help.'

'Buck Radd?' Hart demanded.

'Radd? Hell, no! I got a gal and her young brother in town. They showed up a couple of days ago in a wagon with their dead parents aboard. Seems they were attacked by several men in Mesquite Valley and their parents shot down in cold blood.'

'I met them just after the shooting.' Hart's expression was impassive. 'I was trailing Buck Radd at the time, and from the description of the men the girl gave me I'm sure Radd was responsible for the killing. I'm here now because I've trailed Radd in. I think he's in the town, and I mean to smoke him out before daylight.'

'Jeez! Radd here? He's a real killer.

Do you reckon he's come in to get the Harmon gal and her brother?'

'Have you heard any shooting since darkness fell?' Hart countered.

'No, thank God.' Walker shook his head. Sweat beaded his forehead and he was plainly uneasy.

'I'll take a look around,' Hart said. 'You won't have any trouble from Radd if I can spot him before he sees me.'

'I'll go with you,' Walker offered.

'No. I'll do it alone, but come running if you hear shooting.'

'OK.' Walker sat down at his desk and Hart departed.

Cottonwood Creek was a one-street town. The buildings were made of adobe, all one-storey with false façades, except for the two-storey hotel. Shadows were dense where beams of lamplight failed to reach, and Hart walked slowly along the street to the saloon, situated beside the general store. He peered into the smoky interior of the low building; saw more than a dozen men present, and studied faces

116

before entering. Buck Radd would be easy to identify with his scarred face, and he was not present.

Hart knew most of the men by sight and stood at a corner of the bar, checking out the big room, his hand close to the butt of his holstered gun. The 'tender approached with a smile of welcome on his leathery face. He was tall and thin and his completely bald head shone in the lamplight.

'Howdy, Hart?' he greeted. 'What brings you into our part of the country?'

'Hi, Curly. I'm looking for Buck Radd. Do you know him by sight?'

'I've seen a dodger on him. He's an ugly cuss with that scar. I ain't seen him around, and anyone coming into town would pass through here. We ain't had any trouble for a long time; not since you killed Herb Warner out there in the street.'

'I remember it.' Hart nodded. 'Gimme a beer and then I'll make a round of the town.'

A tall glass of root-beer came sliding

in front of Hart and he drank it slowly, thinking about Radd. When he had finished the beer he left the saloon and stood in the shadows in front the batwings, listening and looking around. He was about to move on when the sound of hurried footsteps came to him and he glanced to his right to see a slight figure approaching at a run along the sidewalk. Even as he recognized the figure as female he spotted a man moving fast in pursuit of the girl.

She was breathless, and lamplight falling upon her face from a saloon window showed Hart that she was frightened. He reached out a big left hand and grasped her left arm as she reached him, pulling her up in mid-stride. She fell against him, moaning in fright.

'Help me!' she gasped, trying to straighten. 'Radd, the outlaw, is after me! He's going to kill me.'

Hart looked over the girl's head at the approaching man just as the newcomer entered the light issuing from the saloon window. Shock hit him like a blow from a sledge hammer. It was Buck Radd. He saw the disfiguring scar on the outlaw's face, and reached for his pistol as the outlaw came up. The girl was in view but Hart was back in the shadows. Radd reached out a long arm, his fingers crooking into a claw to seize the girl. Hart stepped forward a pace to meet him, the muzzle of his levelled pistol thrusting into Radd's stomach.

'Got you, Radd,' Hart said exultantly. 'Stick 'em up and stand still. I got you dead to rights.'

Radd was taken completely by surprise, but his reflexes were honed to an unnatural sharpness by his way of life. His right hand swept in and thrust against Hart's pistol while he twisted to his left and attempted to stay out of the line of fire. Hart lifted his left hand and delivered a solid blow with his clenched fist that struck the bandit on the jaw. Radd staggered, his right hand snaking towards his holstered gun. Hart brought up his own weapon and slammed the long barrel against the side of Radd's head.

The gang boss fell to the ground instantly. Hart bent over him and pulled the man's pistol from its holster. He straightened, grinning exultantly.

'It's OK, Miss Harmon,' he said briskly. 'I've laid him low. He won't trouble you now. Come with me while I stick him behind bars, and then we can talk.'

He released his hold on the girl's arm and she staggered; would have fallen had he not grasped her again. He held her steady with his strong left arm while he covered the inert figure of Buck Radd lying on the sidewalk, unable to believe that after his days of fruitlessly hunting the elusive outlaw, Radd should walk into him so easily.

'Radd surprised me in the hotel,' Cindy gasped. 'I'd been having nightmares about him, and suddenly, he was here in the flesh.'

'He won't scare anyone where he's

going,' Hart responded, glancing around over the girl's head. Radd was beginning to stir. 'Follow me to the jail.'

He bent over Radd and grasped the man to raise him to his feet. At that precise moment a gun blasted from the shadows along the sidewalk. Hart felt a slug tug at his hat-brim and he dropped to one knee instinctively, his pistol swinging up to reply. That was when Radd made his bid to escape.

The outlaw threw a right-hand punch that came out of the darkness and crashed against Hart's jaw with exploding force. Hart, caught unawares, took the full power of the blow. He fell forward on to his face, and was barely aware of making contact with the sidewalk. The girl's voice rang out sharply in a shrill cry, which Hart's ears registered just before total blackness enveloped him, and then his senses cut out.

6

Hart came to his senses slowly to find himself still gripping his pistol. He raised his head and looked around, frowning as he collected his scattered wits. There was no sign of Buck Radd, and Cindy Harmon was gone also. He groaned and staggered to his feet, levelling his .45 when he heard the sound of running footsteps coming towards him. There was a buzzing in his ears, and he recalled that a shot had been fired at him from the shadows of the street — had been so close it clipped the brim of his hat.

Leaning back against the wall beside the batwings, Hart took stock of his surroundings. A man was approaching slowly now, lamplight reflecting from the law star on his chest and the gun in his hand.

'Are you OK, Hart?' Walker called. 'I heard a shot.

'Radd was here.' Hart shook his head. 'He was after Cindy Harmon.'

He explained what had occurred and Walker cursed.

'What I don't understand is the shot that was fired,' Hart mused 'Radd came into town alone and ran into my hands, but somewhere along the line he picked up someone who was backing him up.'

'It's a fact that Radd has a lot of friends in the county.' Walker holstered his gun. 'We'd better go right through the town searching for him. I ain't heard the sound of horses leaving, so he can't be far away.'

'And the girl.' Hart grimaced as he thought of her. 'She was scared out of her wits. Where is she? Surely Radd wouldn't take her along with him?'

Several men were standing just inside the saloon, peering over the batwings.

'I saw a man out here with a girl,' one of them said. 'He had her by the arm, and they went off in the direction of the livery barn. The girl didn't object to him, and there was no one else with them. I didn't see a second man, but there was a gun-flash from across the street.'

Hart started along the sidewalk, holding his pistol, and Walker followed closely. They entered the livery barn but found no sign of Radd or the girl. Hart fought impatience as he began a search of the town, aware that he could do nothing beyond looking around until dawn came. By that time the outlaw would be miles away. An hour's meticulous searching revealed nothing, as Hart had expected, and he and Walker returned to the law office.

'Hey!' Walker exclaimed as he sat down at his desk. He looked up at Hart, his face alive with sudden hope. 'What's happened to the Harmon boy? We didn't see him anywhere in town. He should be in the hotel.'

Hart nodded and turned to the door. Walker joined him and they hurried along to the hotel. The night-clerk gave them the number of the room Hal Harmon was using and they went up to it. The door was locked and there was no response when Hart knocked loudly. The clerk had followed them up the stairs, and produced a pass-key, unlocked the door and pushed it open.

Gun in hand, Hart stalked into the room, and paused when he saw Hal Harmon lying hogtied on the bed. The youth was gagged with a yellow neckerchief, and his eyes were wide as he struggled to get free of his bonds. Walker hurried to the bed and untied the youngster.

'Radd has got Cindy,' Hal cried, springing up from the bed. He grabbed up a Winchester that was leaning against the wall beside the bed. Hart put out a restraining hand as the youngster made a dash for the door.

'Hold it,' he rapped, taking the rifle from the boy. 'We've searched the town and there's no sign of Radd or your sister. Tell me what happened here.'

'Cindy was with me.' Hal spoke in a worried tone. 'We were talking about going back East. There was a knock at the door, and when Cindy answered it, Radd and another man came into the room. Radd had a pistol in his hand. The other man hogtied me, and when they left they took Cindy with them.'

'There was someone with Radd?' Hart's interest quickened. 'Do you know Radd by sight? Did you recognize him?'

'I sure did! I'll never forget him! I've seen his scarred face in my dreams ever since he killed Ma and Pa.'

'So let's talk about the second man,' Hart suggested. 'What was he like?'

'He was a big man! Looked like a giant — big, fat, ugly face and dark, cunning eyes. He was wearing a faded blue shirt, and I saw a bright star-shape in the cloth on his chest, as if he'd worn a law badge out in the sun for a long time before taking it off. The shirt had faded to pale blue, but the star shape was darker.'

'A law badge!' Hart glanced at the intent expression on Walker's face. 'Are there any other deputies around here beside you, Lew?'

Walker shook his head. 'Nope, and certainly no one of the boy's description. The only deputy in the county I know who comes anywhere near to that size is Bull Santee, and I ain't seen him around here in a coon's age.'

'Santee!' Hart was shocked. 'Heck, he was in San Fedora with a couple of hardcases when I left there. He must have followed me here. But how did he get into Radd's company? And what's he up to, working openly with a known outlaw?'

'I wouldn't be surprised at anything Santee does!' Walker shook his head. 'What are you going to do, Hart?'

'Sleep until daylight,' Hart mused. 'I'm certain Radd has left town, and he's taken Cindy Harmon with him. I need to look for their tracks in the morning.'

'Can I ride with you?' Hal demanded. His boyish face was filled with concern, and hatred for Radd shone in his eyes.

Hart studied the youth's hard expression, noted his tension, and nodded. He saw Hal's expression change.

'I'll need you along in case I run into that big man you described,' Hart said. 'If you can identify him on the spot it will save me a lot of time and effort. Try and get some sleep now, and be ready to ride out of town as soon as it gets light. Have you got a horse?'

'I can use one of our harness horses,' Hal said eagerly. 'I've often ridden him when he ain't pulling the wagon.'

'OK. Be at the livery barn when the sun comes up. I'll be ready to ride out the minute it is light enough to see tracks.'

'I'll be ready,' Hal promised. 'I won't be able to sleep again until Cindy is back. If Radd harms her you won't need to arrest him. I'll shoot his eyes out.'

'Well, I need some sleep,' Hart said, 'and if I don't get enough I'll feel like all hell in the morning.'

He left the hotel, and Walker accompanied him to the jail. Hart bedded down in an empty cell, went to sleep almost immediately, and was awake as the first rays of sunlight came peeping into the building through an outside window. Walker was already on the move, and had hot coffee on the stove. Hart declined breakfast. He was impatient to look for tracks, and the town marshal followed him as he went along the street to the saloon.

Hart stood in front of the batwings to look around. He estimated the position of the man who had backed Radd the night before and crossed the street to check the ground. There were boot-prints in the dust but he learned nothing from them.

'I'll be riding out now,' he told Walker.

'I hope you get Radd,' the town marshal said. 'And if you find it was Santee backing that outlaw then I hope you'll gut-shoot him.'

'Santee will get what's coming to him,' Hart promised, and went along the street to the stable.

Hal Harmon was waiting by the

water-trough, his horse ready for travel. The youngster's face looked strained but there was determination in the set of his jaw. Hart greeted the youth, and then cast around for hoof-prints in the dust while Hal watched him silently.

Hart located the tracks of Radd's horse heading off back in the direction of San Fedora, accompanied by two other horses. Hart dropped to one knee and checked the prints closely, and was disappointed when he did not recognize either of the two sets of tracks accompanying Radd as belonging to Santee's horse.

Hart went into the livery barn and saddled his black horse. He led the way out of town and, on reaching the open trail, sent his mount along at a mile-eating run. The tracks they were following were heading straight into the south-west.

Noon came and went, and still Hart pushed on. He questioned Hal as they rode, but elicited little else about Radd. The killing of the boy's parents had been cold-blooded, but Hart was only too aware of the outlaw's evil propensity for murder.

Late afternoon brought a change to the situation. Hart was watching the tracks carefully as they progressed across the range, and his keen gaze spotted one set of prints leading off at an angle to the other two. He halted, got down and checked them. His eyes glinted when he found that Radd was leaving the two riders who had accompanied him from Cottonwood Creek. Those two were keeping to the original direction, looking as if they were heading for San Fedora, and Hart stood for some moments considering the situation, although he knew without having to think about it that his priority was to follow Buck Radd.

'My sister is going on with that big man, isn't she?' Hal asked, his expression showing troubled thoughts.

'That's right.' Hart was tight-lipped.

'And you're going after the outlaw.' Hal shook his head. 'I think that's wrong. We should rescue Cindy before she is harmed.'

'My duty is clear, Hal.' Hart suppressed a sigh. 'I have to stop Radd in his tracks. I came into the county to take care of him, and I'm afraid your sister will have to wait until Radd is back in custody.'

'I can see the tracks their horses are leaving,' Hal said firmly. 'I'll follow them until you catch up.'

'All you'll probably succeed in doing is getting yourself killed.' Hart shook his head. 'You'd better ride with me. With a bit of luck we won't be far behind by sundown. It looks to me like your sister is being taken into San Fedora.'

'No.' Hal shook his head and gigged his mount forward. 'I know where my duty lies.'

Hart mounted and sat his saddle, watching the youngster moving out. He turned his horse to follow Buck Radd's tracks, pushing along at a faster pace.

Nightfall found him still riding. He continued until darkness covered the tracks, when he reined in, aware that he would have to camp until morning. He looked around for a campsite, and was about to unsaddle when his keen gaze caught the dim glow of lamplight ahead in the unbroken blackness of the night. He swung back into his saddle without conscious thought and moved on, hope raising its head in his taut mind. Radd had evidently known there was a habitation out here.

As the light grew in size and brightness, Hart slowed his progress to avoid betraying his presence. He came upon a narrow stream meandering across a level stretch of grassland and dismounted, pausing only to wrap his reins around a low branch of a cottonwood. He braced his wide shoulders as he studied the square of yellow light, which he could see now was issuing from a window in a large cabin.

Moving slowly, Hart made a circuit of the cabin, staying well out from the building to avoid alerting the occupants to his presence. He came upon a low barn to the rear, and heard a horse stamp inside but remained at a distance from it, aware that its owner could be bedded down beside the horse, and there was no way he could gain an edge in the darkness.

Hart moved back to the cabin. He stood in the deep shadows at its rear, listening intently, but could hear no sound through the thick wall. Edging forward a foot at a time, he moved around the cabin until he reached the front right-hand corner, and then stood motionless for several minutes, looking around and listening intently. A keen breeze was blowing into his face. The silence, like a blank wall surrounding him, cut off all sense of reality.

He slid sideways to the lighted window and craned forward to peer into the cabin, and his breath hissed from between his taut lips when he saw an old man seated on a chair against the back wall — tied to the chair, and with blood running down his face from a wound on his forehead. He was only semi-conscious, his head lolling sideways and eye lids flickering.

Hart drew his gun. A man was seated at a table to the right, eating wolfishly from a plate stacked high with food. A tall, thin woman, well past middle age, was also seated at the table, her hands held to her weathered face, her grey hair gleaming in the lamplight. Hart recognized Buck Radd without difficulty. The gang boss had placed his deadly pistol on the table beside his plate, its black muzzle gaping at the woman, and he was eating as if there was no tomorrow.

Without pausing to think about the situation, Hart raised his pistol and crashed the barrel through the window pane. Glass shattered and tinkled. Radd leapt up from his seat, grabbing up his pistol as he did so. Hart did not get a chance to warn Radd to surrender, so fast was the man's movements. He saw Radd's gun swinging up to cover the window and set his own weapon into action. He squeezed the trigger, blasting out the heavy silence, and gun smoke flared around him.

Hart wanted Radd alive, and aimed for the right shoulder. He saw the outlaw stagger under the impact of the heavy .45 slug, but Radd was not a man to surrender without resistance. He dropped to one knee and used both hands to lift his pistol.

'Drop it, Radd,' Hart yelled.

Desperation showed on Radd's face. His mouth was agape. His eyes bulged with shock He brought his pistol up to cover the window and Hart triggered his gun again, before the outlaw's weapon could level at him. The speeding bullet smashed into Radd's pistol, blasting the flesh and bone of his right hand. Radd lost his grip on the gun and sank to his knees, blood spurting from his shattered fingers.

The thunder of the shots faded quickly. Hart remained at the window, covering Radd. The woman was frozen in shock on her seat. Hart drew a deep breath and exhaled slowly. Radd was his prisoner again, and this time he would ensure that the outlaw could not escape justice.

Hart yawned to dispel the tension in his ears and head.

'Lady,' he called, 'pick up that pistol and then make sure the cabin door is unbarred. I'm a Texas Ranger, and that man is Buck Radd, an outlaw. Get up now and do like I say.'

The woman did not move, such was her shock, and the man tied to the chair called to her urgently, insistently. She started nervously as his voice cut through her bemused senses, and then she got to her feet, picked up Radd's discarded pistol, and went to the cabin door. Hart heard the wooden bar being removed. He still covered Radd, who was sitting on the floor holding his right hand with his left as he tried to stanch the flow of blood from his mangled fingers.

Hart went to the door of the cabin as it swung open and entered quickly. Radd was too occupied with his damaged hand to care about what was going on around him. Hart put away his gun and grasped Radd by the shoulders. He hauled the outlaw to his feet and dumped him on a chair.

'Sit still and don't give me any trouble or I'll gutshoot you,' Hart warned. He crossed the room and untied the bound man, and then went back to Radd. 'Have you got any other weapons on you?' he demanded.

'Look at my hand!' Radd snarled. 'You've busted it.'

'You're lucky I didn't put a slug through your head.' Hart searched Radd and relieved the outlaw of a knife and a .41 derringer.

'Thank God you showed up when you did,' the man said, rubbing his wrists. 'I'm Joe Williams, and that's my wife Martha. This man came in here asking for food, and got the drop on me. He said he was gonna kill us before he left.'

'And he would have done so,' Hart replied. 'But his killing days are over now. He's slated for the hangman's rope. If you've got anything to bind Radd's wounds, I'll be obliged. I wouldn't want him to bleed to death and cheat justice.'

The woman produced cloth, and Hart tended Radd's wounds.

'There's nothing I can do about the hand,' Hart said after inspecting the limb. 'I'll bind it and we'll head for San Fedora. The shoulder wound is clean. The bullet passed clear through without touching bone. Why did you kidnap Cindy Harmon from Cottonwood Creek, Radd?'

'She saw me and was gonna tell the law,' Radd grated. 'I should've killed her and her brother when I killed her folks.'

'Who is the big man you left her with on the trail?' Hart enquired. 'It looked to me like he's taking her on to San Fedora. What's behind all the traipsin' around you've done lately? And tell me about Sam Straker. Why did you have him shot down?'

'I've gone as far as I can with Straker.

139

He was fixin' to tell the law about me. I couldn't get him to see reason no more, so he had to go.'

'He ain't dead yet, so don't write him off. He's a tough old wolf, and I reckon he'll be around to see you swing. Why did you leave San Fedora for Cottonwood Creek, and what's the name of the big man who backed you in Cottonwood Creek? Where's he taking Cindy Harmon now?'

'Why don't you ask him who he is?' Radd countered. 'You're asking too many questions, Ranger.'

'I'll talk to him when I catch up with him.' Hart fashioned a rough sling and put it around Radd's neck. The outlaw cursed when he eased his right hand into it. 'You'll do until we reach San Fedora,' Hart commented. 'Come on, we'll split the breeze now.'

'I can't ride!' Radd protested.

'You can walk if you fancy it,' Hart replied roughly. 'On your feet, and don't get any ideas about jumping me. I'd like an excuse to kill you.'

Joe Williams picked up a lamp and led the way out to the barn. He saddled Radd's horse, and Hart helped the outlaw into his saddle. He took his leave of Williams and walked to the spot where he had left his horse. He was filled with a sense of urgent concern for Cindy Harmon, and yet he was aware that he could not resume the trail until daylight, although he realized the danger the girl was in.

He rode several miles from the Williamses' cabin before stopping for the night, bedding Radd down, hand-cuffing the outlaw despite Radd's protests about his wounds. Then he settled down yards away from Radd, and slept without incident until dawn lightened the sky. By the time the sun showed over the eastern horizon he was ready to ride, and when he reached the spot where he had parted from Hal Harmon he put the black forward at a fast clip, leading Radd's horse.

They rode in silence. Radd was pale-faced, badly shocked by his wounds, and the jolting saddle filled him with agony, but Hart did not heed his prisoner's complaints about the ride and continued at a fast clip. The tracks were plain on the ground and they made good time.

Hart came to the spot where Hal Harmon had made camp for the night, and rode on determinedly, watching his surroundings, ready for trouble, and ever alert for anything Radd might try, although the outlaw seemed too badly hurt even to consider escaping. The morning passed, and it became obvious to Hart that the tracks were heading for San Fedora.

He wondered at the identity of the big man who had backed Radd in Cottonwood Creek. Bull Santee fitted the description, but Hart maintained an open mind. He would know soon enough, he told himself. They were only a few miles from town, where he expected to find the answers to several of the questions bothering him.

Later, Hart reined in quickly when he

breasted a rise and saw a horse grazing in the brush ahead. The animal was saddled, although there was no sign of its rider. Hart recognized the animal as the one Hal Harmon had ridden, and went forward cautiously, hand close to the butt of his holstered gun.

He reached the grazing horse and dismounted, warning Radd to remain inactive. He was aware that the outlaw watched him closely as he checked the horse and then looked around more closely for Hal Harmon. A pistol shot rang out, tossing a string of echoes to the horizon, and Hart heard the crackle of a bullet passing high over his head. He saw a puff of gunsmoke drifting on the breeze some yards away and hurried towards it, gun in hand.

Hal Harmon was lying in the brush. His eyes were closed and there was blood on his chest. Hart hurried to the youngster's side, filled with apprehension. The youth had been dry-gulched, and looked to be in a bad way.

7

Hal Harmon opened his eyes, and relief showed in his face when he recognized Hart, who dropped to his knees by the youngster's side and quickly checked his wound. Hal, hit in the chest high on the left side, had lost a great deal of blood. He tried to speak but his words were badly slurred, and he fell silent and closed his eyes while Hart attended to him.

'It's pretty bad,' Hart commented at length. 'Tell me what happened, Hal.'

'A bullet came out of the brush and knocked me out of my saddle,' the youngster mumbled. 'I didn't see anything, and heard nothing except the shot. I must have been unconscious for hours. I figure it was the man with Cindy who shot me.'

'I'll look around for tracks.' Hart sat back on his heels. 'I've done all I can for you, Hal, and I'm gonna have to leave you lying here while I ride to San Fedora and get the doc to come out and pick you up.'

'Sure. Do what you have to, and try to find Cindy and the big man before you bother about me.'

Hart made the youngster as comfortable as possible and then took his leave. He mounted, took up the reins of Radd's horse, and moved out, his eyes studying the ground. Fifty yards out from Hal's position, he cast around for tracks, and came eventually to a spot where two horses had stood for some considerable time. A camp had been made — there were the remains of a small fire, and Hart shook his head as he looked around. Hal had been unlucky enough to stumble upon the man holding Cindy prisoner.

The hoof-prints tallied with two of the three sets of prints Hart had followed from Cottonwood Creek, and he pushed on faster, following the tracks towards San Fedora. Radd remained silent, teeth clenched against the pain of his wounds, and he seemed to have slipped into a kind of semi-consciousness that was related to shock. Hart felt no sympathy for the outlaw.

It was nearing noon when San Fedora appeared on the skyline, and Hart noted that the tracks he was following turned off to the left just before he hit the street. They made a half-circle behind the buildings on the left side of the street, and he ascertained their general direction before heading for the law office.

'Hurry up and get the doc to me,' Radd said through clenched teeth as Hart dismounted in front of the jail. 'I ain't done yet, Hart, and you've got a lot of grief coming to you when I get free. You'll pay a big bill when it comes to a reckoning.'

Hart ignored the outlaw and dragged Radd from his saddle. Radd cursed and groaned in pain but Hart was unmoved by the man's condition and half-carried

146

him across the sidewalk and into the law office. Frank Burnside was emerging from the cell block as Hart crossed the threshold of the office, and came forward quickly when he recognized Radd.

'You got him!' Burnside exclaimed, pulling forward a chair.

'Yeah, but not before he helled around some more.' Hart lowered Radd on to the chair and straightened, explaining all that had occurred since he had ridden out of San Fedora. 'Is Bull Santee still in town?'

'Those two hardcases Santee rode in with are still here, but Santee pulled up just after you did. I reckoned he went back to Bleak Ridge. Don't tell me he trailed you and gave you trouble.'

'Yeah. I guess he did. Put Radd behind bars and get the doctor to him. I'll take a look around town before heading out with a wagon to pick up Hal Harmon.'

Hart waited until Radd was safely behind bars before leaving to search for

Santee and Cindy. When he walked into the saloon and saw Santee's two side-kicks seated at a table he drew his gun and crossed to them. Both men stiffened as he approached, and one dropped his right hand below the table.

'You're asking for a slug between the eyes,' Hart warned. The man lifted his hand quickly and placed it on the table top. 'Where's Santee?'

'He headed back to Bleak Ridge to talk some with the sheriff.'

'What colour shirt was Santee wearing when he left you?' Hart asked.

The two men exchanged glances.

'What kind of a question is that?' one demanded.

'Pick a colour, and it better be the right one,' Hart warned.

'Blue,' the other man said. 'What's on your mind?'

'When Santee left here why wasn't he riding his own horse?' Hart persisted.

'His horse was lame so he borrowed mine.'

'What's your name?' Hart did not

relax his vigilance, and his pistol covered both men.

'I'm Ben Gatting, and he's Cal Wenn.'

'So what are you doing riding around with Santee?'

'Sheriff Bland made us special deputies and sent us with Santee to help track down Buck Radd,' Wenn said.

'We're on the side of the law,' Gatting added.

'That's more than you can say for Santee.' Hart motioned with his pistol. 'Get up and lift your hands. I'm arresting the pair of you until I get the chance to check you out. Santee didn't go back to Bleak Ridge, so tell me what he said to you before he rode out.'

'As far as we know, he was going to see Sheriff Bland,' Gatting insisted. 'We ain't done nothing wrong.'

'Santee rode back here about five hours ago,' Hart replied. 'I followed his tracks all the way from Cottonwood Creek. How did Santee know where to go to contact Buck Radd in Cottonwood Creek?'

Both men remained silent, and Hart ordered them to their feet. He disarmed them and took them along to the jail. Burnside locked them in a cell. The doctor was in the cell occupied by Buck Radd and Hart paused by the open door.

'How is Sam Straker doing, Doc?' Hart enquired,

'He'll pull through but it looks like being a long job. He's got a room in the hotel and Beth is nursing him.' Doc Crane did not look up from his ministrations.

'I've got a wagon standing by to go out for the wounded youngster,' Burnside said.

'We've got something else to do before I can ride out.' Hart explained the situation, and took Burnside with him to check out the tracks left by the two horses he had been following.

They located the tracks on the back lots and found them making for the rear of the livery barn. Hart led the way into the barn, his pistol drawn. There

150

were a dozen horses in the stalls inside and Hart checked on them while Burnside stood looking around alertly. Hart paused beside a roan and patted its nose.

'This looks like the horse Gatting was riding when he came into town with Santee, and he said Santee borrowed it because his buckskin was lame. That was why I didn't see the tracks of Santee's horse around Cottonwood Creek.'

He checked the animal's hoofs, and was satisfied that it had made the tracks he had followed from Cottonwood Creek. He looked over the horse occupying the next stall, checked its hoofs, and nodded, certain that it was the animal Cindy Harmon had ridden. But where were Santee and the girl now? Hart realized that he had to find out the hard way and search the town for the girl's whereabouts. He needed to locate Cindy and tie up some loose ends.

'You said Santee caused trouble the

last time he was in town,' Hart mused as they left the stable. Burnside nodded.

'You can say that again. He latched on to Mamie Coe, a widow who runs the dress-shop next to the general store, and that caused him to step on the toes of Hank Toone, who was fixing to ask Mamie to marry him. Toone owns the saloon, and he raised a ruckus with Santee that got out of hand. Santee tried to settle it in his usual way — he's only got one answer to resistance and that's to use his fists. But he got more than he bargained for. Toone backed his play with two bouncers he employs at the saloon, and Santee took off back to Bleak Ridge and stayed away. I was surprised when he showed up here again the other day.'

'And did Toone wed Mamie?' Hart asked.

'Nope. He broke all contact with her, and Mamie has kept out of the limelight since.'

'I'd better have a word with her,'

Hart decided. 'Santee must be holed up somewhere around here, and I need to dig him out to talk to him. I'd leave you to handle him because I need to get back to Hal Harmon, but Santee might turn nasty when he's confronted so I'll have to see this through before I can consider doing anything else.'

'I'll come with you,' Burnside said. 'Mamie will talk to me, but I don't think she has anything to do with Santee these days. I'm sure she hates him after what happened between them. By the way, I did some checking around town after you left and found that one of the hardcases Hallam keeps around left town suddenly. His name is Mason, and I heard he rode out to the BH ranch that Hallam owns, west of here. I got the feeling he went to conceal the fact that he stopped your slug the other night. I talked to Dunne, Hallam's other hardcase, but he was cagey, and that made me even more suspicious.'

'Why does Hallam need a couple of

hardcases around?' Hart questioned, frowning. He shrugged and shook his head. 'We'll have to leave Hallam and his hardcases until we've got on top of what's happened to Santee and Cindy Harmon,' he decided.

They walked along the street to the dress-shop, and entered the establishment to find Mamie Coe chatting with a female customer. Hart studied the big woman whom Burnside addressed as Mamie. She was over-large, obese. He judged her to be in her early forties, and she possessed a certain gracefulness despite her bulk. She studied Hart with narrowed blue eyes when Burnside introduced him, and offered him a small, fleshy hand to shake. Her grip was surprisingly strong, and her voice, when she spoke, gave Hart to suppose that she was from one of the Northern states.

'I haven't set eyes on Santee in months,' she said when Hart acquainted her with the situation, 'and if I do see him, knowing that you want him, I'll inform you immediately.' Her voice shook a little. She could not take her eyes off Hart, and he saw tiny beads of sweat break out on her upper lip. She shook her head, her nervousness obvious, but she made a big effort to regain her poise. 'Truth to tell, I think I am the last person in town he would visit at this time.'

'It was a forlorn hope that he might have contacted you,' Hart said. 'I think he must be hiding in town, and we have to check everyone who knows him.'

'You can search my private rooms over the shop,' Mamie said in a breathless tone, and gulped nervously as she glanced up at the low ceiling. 'Believe me, I have nothing to hide.'

'I believe you.' Hart smiled, anxious to put her at ease. 'We'll check right through the town before we start getting concerned about Santee.'

They left the shop and paused on the sidewalk.

'Mamie sure looked guilty as hell about something,' Hart said. 'I'll bet she knows where Santee is, but I don't think she would hide him up in her place.'

'We can check,' Burnside said eagerly. 'There's a flight of steps in the alley that leads to the apartment over the shop.'

'If Santee is up there then he'll keep,' Hart decided. 'We'll leave it until nightfall. Right now I'd better get moving to bring in Hal Harmon.'

'OK I'll keep an eye on Mamie and the shop. Do you want me to pick up Santee, if I see him?'

'It might be better just to watch him — find out where he holes up. If we catch him with Cindy Harmon then he'll have a lot of explaining to do.'

Burnside moved away, then paused when Beth Straker appeared in the doorway of the hotel. Hart noted that Brent Hallam was with the girl, and he subjected the hotelier to an intent scrutiny.

'How's Sam?' Hart called.

'Doc says he'll live, but we have to keep him quiet. It will be a long job, though, and I suspect Sam will give up the Double S when he's on his feet again.'

'Has he said so?' Hart frowned. 'He doesn't look to be the type that quits. I have to ride out but I'll be back later today, and I'll need to talk to Sam soon as I can get around to it.'

'He's conscious but very weak.' Beth shook her head. 'I don't think he's up to talking. The doctor said he shouldn't see anyone just yet. It would be better if you can leave him as long as possible.'

'I'll bear that in mind.' Hart moved on to the law office, where a buckboard was standing hitched and ready to roll. An old man was sitting on the seat of the vehicle, and roused himself when Hart approached.

'I'm Frank Valera,' the oldster said. 'I own the livery barn. Are you the one who wants the buck-board?'

'Sure.' Hart gave him directions for finding Hal Harmon. 'Get moving now. I'll catch up with you before you get too

157

far ahead and lead you to the spot.'

Valera shook his reins and turned the buckboard around in the wide street. Hart watched for a moment, and wished he could be in more than one place at a time. He thought over the situation and decided that he was doing the right thing. Radd was in jail, with several of his men, and Hal Harmon had to be brought in for treatment. He unhitched his horse, swung into the saddle, and set out after the buckboard, aware that he needed to be back in town by sunset.

Hal Harmon was unconscious when Hart dismounted beside the youngster, but stirred when Hart bent over him. Lying out in the hot sun had not helped Hal's condition, and Hart uncorked his canteen and administered some of its contents to the youth. The buckboard arrived and they placed Hal on a pile of straw in the back.

'I can find my way back to town if you need to be getting on,' Valera said.

Hart squinted at the sky and shook

his head. 'I'll ride in the wagon,' he decided.

He tied his horse to the back of the buckboard and climbed into the vehicle to hunker down beside Hal. Valera whipped his team and they started back to San Fedora.

The sun was sitting on the western horizon by the time the buckboard reached town, and shadows were closing in on the clustered buildings when they stopped outside the doctor's office. Hart waited until the doctor took charge of Hal before leading his horse to the stable. He took care of the animal methodically before considering his own needs, and then entered the saloon for a drink to wash the dust from his throat. Afterwards, he went along to the law office.

Frank Burnside arose eagerly from his desk when Hart walked in on him.

'I've been getting a mite impatient since the sun went down' Burnside said. 'I reckon we should have looked inside Mamie's apartment when she finished in the shop.'

'Let's pay her a visit now,' Hart said.

They left the office, Burnside pausing to lock the office door. Full darkness covered the town and stars were twinkling in the black stretch of the sky.

'I'm gonna need to bring in some extra men to guard this place while Radd and his hardcases are behind bars,' Burnside commented.

'I wish you would. Radd busted out of jail in Bleak Ridge after I'd arrested him, and I don't want to have to chase him again.'

They walked along the street to the dress-shop. The darkness was split by yellow lamplight issuing from various windows, and Hart noted lights showing in Mamie's apartment above the dress-shop. Hart led the way, feeling for the steps to the apartment with his feet and ascending quietly. He reached the door at the top and tried it with a cautious hand. It was locked. He drew his pistol before knocking.

'Come on, Mamie,' Burnside said at

Hart's elbow when the knock went unanswered.

Hart rapped on the centre panel of the door with the muzzle of his pistol, and echoes fled through the night. Silence pressed in around them as tense moments passed, and then Mamie called from the other side of the door.

'Who's there?'

'It's Ranger Hart, and Frank Burnside, ma'am. We need to talk to you.'

'I don't open my door after dark,' Mamie replied. 'You'll have to come back in the morning.'

'I must talk to you now,' Hart insisted. 'Please open the door.'

'Come on, Mamie. Open up,' Burnside said. 'There's nothing to be afraid of.'

There was no reply, and impatience began to grow inside Hart. He was beginning to consider kicking in the door when he heard bolts being withdrawn on the inside, then the door was opened a crack and Mamie's desperate face showed in the opening.

'What do you want?' she demanded. 'I've had a busy day and I'm very tired.'

'We won't keep you long,' Hart said. 'May we come in?'

'I'm about to take a bath,' Mamie protested, 'and the water is getting cold.'

Hart placed his left hand on the door and pushed gently. Mamie retreated before his advance, uttering a string of protests until Hart stood on the threshold, his big pistol levelled at the hip as he looked around the room. Mamie fell silent and stood motionless, her eyes downcast.

Hart looked around quickly. There was no sign of Santee. Two doors leading out of the room were both closed, and he returned his attention to the uneasy woman.

'Is there anyone up here with you, Mamie?' Burnside asked. He walked across to the door on the left and opened it to reveal a small kitchen, which was unoccupied. He threw a glance at Hart as he moved towards the other door.

'That's my bedroom.' Mamie hurried to place her back to the closed door.

'We need to take a look,' Hart insisted. 'We're searching the whole town, and have to check every place. I'm sorry to distrub you, and if you'll just move aside and stand quiet we'll take a quick peek inside and then leave you in peace. You can't object unless you've got something to hide.'

'My mother is here from New York,' Mamie said nervously, desperation showing in her fleshy face. 'She's not very well, and I won't have her disturbed.'

Burnside grasped Mamie's arm and led her aside. Mamie turned on him, beating at his chest with clenched fists and protesting bitterly. Hart opened the bedroom door. A lamp was burning inside the room, and he cocked his pistol as he entered, half-expecting to see Santee's big figure. Disappointment filled him when he found the room empty, although there was a figure lying in the bed. He eased his hammer forward and returned the big .45 to its holster. He was turning to apologize to Mamie for disturbing her when the woman in the bed raised her head and he saw that she was gagged.

Hart recognized Cindy Harmon and hurried to her side. The girl was bound tightly and he released her. Cindy tried to arise, but her limbs were cramped and Hart had to help her into a sitting position.

'Where is Santee?' Cindy gasped. 'He said he would be back just after dark. He's holding me until Radd gets back.'

'Radd is back,' Hart said. 'He's behind bars, and that's where Santee will be when I find him. Have you any idea where he's gone?'

'He told Mamie he had some checking up to do. I was in fear for my life. He kept threatening me.'

'You're safe now,' Hart soothed. 'Just sit there and relax.' He confronted Mamie, who had subsided into a chair and was holding her hands to her face.

'So what was going on here, Mamie?'

Hart demanded. 'You'd better come clean and tell me all about it.'

'That Santee! He threatened to kill me if I didn't help him out. He said he was desperate because his friends weren't around to help him. I don't know where he's gone, but he said he'd be back soon.'

'That's OK.' Hart nodded. 'We'll wait for him. You better sit in your bedroom until this is over, Mamie, and whatever happens, keep quiet.'

Burnside accompanied Mamie into the back room and returned with Cindy, who was showing the effects of her experiences. She was shaking badly. Hart explained the situation to her and she nodded.

'I've got some bad news for you,' Hart said, and told her about her Hal.

'I must go to him,' Cindy said at once. She straightened and staggered.

'Sure, but not until we've got Santee,' Hart insisted.

They settled down to wait, and time seemed to stand still. Hart bolted the door and paced the room, his face impassive. An hour passed before heavy footsteps sounded on the steps outside. Hart fetched Mamie out of her bedroom and led her to the outer door. A heavy hand pounded on the panel. Mamie's face was ashen and she was trembling uncontrollably. Hart motioned for her to answer.

'Who's there?' Mamie called in a quavering tone.

'Who the hell do you think it is?' Bull Santee replied. 'Open the damn door!'

Hart stepped to his left, drawing his pistol. Burnside entered the kitchen and concealed himself, gun ready. Mamie unbolted the door and Santee thrust it open — came lunging into the room. The opening door covered Hart and he stepped aside as Mamie staggered back several paces. Santee looked around suspiciously, hand on the butt of his holstered gun. His back was to Hart as he confronted Mamie.

'Anyone called here?' Santee demanded.

'We called, and waited for you to

show up, Santee,' Hart said.

Santee moved fast for a big man. He whirled to face Hart, his gun hand lifting his pistol despite his seeing Hart with his weapon already levelled.

'Hold it, Santee,' Burnside yelled from the kitchen doorway.

Santee flung a glance across a broad shoulder, saw Burnside at his back with levelled gun. He grinned mirthlessly as he lifted his hands wide of his body.

'Looks like you got me cold,' he snarled.

'Get your hands up high,' Hart rapped. 'Don't do anything stupid, Santee; because I don't wanta kill you. I've got a lot of questions to ask you. Take his gun, Frank, and shake him down for any other weapons. Then we'll mosey over to your office and get down to some serious work.'

Burnside was grinning as he moved in on Santee. He relieved the shocked deputy of his pistol and then searched the big man to produce a pocket Colt .41 and a long-bladed knife from a sheath on the back of his gunbelt.

'On your way,' Hart ordered. 'You know where the jail is so head for it. We've got a long night ahead of us, Santee.'

Burnside led the way down to the street and Hart stayed close to Santee as they headed for the jail, with Cindy Harmon behind Hart. Santee was docile under the threat of Hart's gun but, although Hart was ready for resistance, the big deputy made a desperate bid to escape as Burnside unlocked the door of the law office.

Santee grasped Burnside, spun him around, and thrust him into Hart, pulling Burnside's pistol from its holster as he did so. Hart was already side-stepping as Burnside collided with him, and missed the full force of the impact. He threw himself headlong to his right, landed on the edge of the sidewalk, and rolled into the street as Santee triggered Burnside's pistol, filling the shadows with gun-flame and battering the silence with blasting noise . . .

8

Hart could hear bullets smacking into the ground around him as he rolled desperately to stay ahead of Santee's aim. His senses began to whirl and he stopped his movement to thrust up his gun hand. Santee was in deep shadow, but the flashes of a pistol marked the man's position, and Hart triggered two quick shots into the gloom. Gun echoes faded slowly. Hart heard the sound of a gun hitting the sidewalk. Then Santee came forward out of the shadows, walking jerkily on stiff legs. He fell like a tree that had been axed, without raising his hands to save his face, and hit the edge of the sidewalk to roll off and sprawl into the thick dust of the street, burrowing forward head first under the impetus of his fall.

Burnside came forward from the left, and bent to pick up his gun, which

Santee had dropped. Hart pushed himself to his feet and looked around for the girl. Cindy was leaning against the front wall of the office, a hand to her mouth and eyes wide in shock.

'Are you OK?' Hart asked her. She nodded wordlessly.

'Santee ain't good.' Burnside straightened from a cursory examination of the big deputy. 'I'd better fetch Doc Crane.'

'Unlock the office before you go,' Hart said, and Burnside swung around to obey before striding off along the sidewalk.

Hart lit the lamp inside the office and returned to the sidewalk. He dropped to one knee beside the massive bulk of the unconscious Santee and examined him. One of his slugs had hit Santee in the chest on his left side, and Hart was relieved to find that it was not a serious wound — no vital organs had been touched But Santee was losing a lot of blood, and Hart pulled his knife, slashed away the front of Santee's blue shirt, and stuffed a dusty corner of it, using a forefinger, into the leaking bullet wound to stanch the bleeding. Santee groaned but did not regain consciousness. Hart regarded the big man without emotion.

Hart turned his attention to Cindy. The girl had not moved. He took her arm, led her into the office, and sat her down at the desk. She was badly shocked by the action, her hands shaking uncontrollably. Hart looked in the right-hand drawer of the desk, located a bottle containing whiskey, and poured a quantity of the liquid into a tin cup. Cindy drank it without protest, and coughed as the raw liquor burned her throat. She leaned back in her seat and closed her eyes.

Hart stood in the doorway looking down at the motionless Santee until boots sounded on the sidewalk. Burnside returned with the doctor, and Crane examined the wounded man.

'He ain't in danger of dying,' Crane said at length. 'Let's get him on the desk in the office and I'll remove the bullet.'

They lifted Santee and carried him into the office; placed him on the desk, and the doctor set about his gory work.

'How's Hal Harmon, Doc?' Hart asked as he peered over the doctor's shoulder at Santee.

'He'll pull through, barring complications.' Crane inserted a probe into the bullet wound in Santee's shoulder. The deputy groaned and stirred but did not open his eyes.

'Can I see Hal?' Cindy demanded. 'He's my brother, Doctor.'

'Sure. You can help nurse him back to health. Give me a few minutes and I'll take you to my place.'

Burnside was standing outside on the sidewalk, talking to a group of townsfolk who had been attracted by the shooting. Hart joined him, reloading his pistol before holstering it. One of the townsmen was talking excitedly and the rest were listening intently.

'Something is going on that ain't right,' the man was saying. 'There was a big bust-up right in the foyer of the hotel, and I heard Beth Straker tell Hallam she would take old Sam back to the Double S soon as it got daylight. Hallam was fit to be tied. I thought he was gonna strike that gal.'

Hart caught Burnside's eye and motioned with his head.

'Can you manage here without me, Frank?' he asked. 'I need to talk to Sam Straker, if he's up to it. Then I'll get me something to eat.'

'Sure.' Burnside nodded. 'I'll keep a couple of these men with me until you get back. Watch your step.'

Hart nodded and went off along the sidewalk. He paused at the batwings of the saloon to peer inside, and was surprised to find the big room almost filled to overflowing. Then it came to him that today was Saturday, which meant that most of the cowboys from the nearby ranches were in town to celebrate the weekend. He walked to the hotel.

Brent Hallam was standing in the lobby, smartly dressed in a dark-blue town-suit, and although he was chatting easily with several well-dressed older men, who had the look of cattle ranchers about them, his face betrayed a mental attitude that was not in keeping with his appearance. His eyes were filled with passion and his lips were pulled against his teeth, as if he had trouble controlling his temper.

Hart walked to the desk, skirting Hallam and the ranchers, and attracted the attention of the woman seated at the reception desk.

'Good evenin', ma'am,' he greeted. 'I wanta talk to Beth Straker. What's her room number?'

'Beth ain't seeing anyone this evening,' Hallam cut in.

Hart shifted his gaze to the hotelier, his face relaxing in a smile.

'It ain't up to Beth whether she sees me or not,' Hart replied. 'I wanta speak to her, and right now. So where is she?'

'She went to bed early.' Hallam's tone was inflexible and there was an edge to his voice which Hart did not miss. 'She's had a lot of worry about Sam and, as he's sleeping peacefully right now, she decided to turn in and get some badly needed rest.'

'That's too bad.' Hart nodded. 'I need to see her now.'

'Are you deaf?' Hallam's tone rose slightly. 'I told you she ain't seeing anyone this evening.'

'There must be something wrong with your ears,' Hart countered. 'Stop right where you are and shut your mouth or I'll slap you behind bars for obstructing a law officer in the execution of his duty.'

Hallam stiffened, and for a moment Hart thought the man was going to push his luck, but the hotelier merely shrugged and returned his attention to the cattlemen. Hart smiled at the receptionist, who was staring at him in shock.

'Well?' he asked.

'Miss Straker is in room eleven. That's up the stairs and to the right.'

Hart nodded and turned to the stairs.

He ascended, turned into the corridor at the top, and dropped his gun hand to the butt of his holstered pistol when he saw a big man dressed in a brown store-suit sitting on a chair outside one of the rooms. The man got to his feet as Hart approached, and Hart saw that he was outside room eleven.

The guard was a big man with a lumpy face, his nose misshapen and his small eyes peering out of dark circles of puffy flesh that had been battered considerably at some time in the past. He was well over six feet in height, his shoulders massive, his hands like great lumps of beef, with prominent, bony knuckles and thick fingers. His right hand hovered above the butt of a pistol protruding from the holster on his gunbelt, and he gazed intently at Hart as the Ranger approached him, his puffy face changing expression when he realized Hart was making for the room he was guarding.

Hart halted just out of arm's length. He was not quite as tall as the guard, and the man outweighed him by some forty pounds.

'What are you doing here?' Hart demanded.

'I'm Buck Dunne. I work for Hallam,' the man replied hoarsely, 'and I got orders to see no one disturbs Miss Straker tonight. Who in hell are you, and what do you want?'

Hart twitched aside the lapel of his leather vest to reveal his Ranger badge, and the man gazed at it without reaction.

'I'm a Texas Ranger, in case you don't know what the badge means,' Hart said, 'and it means I can go where I want when I want, and see whom I please, and I don't take orders from anyone. Right now I want to see Beth Straker, and you're standing in my way. Step aside, mister. Hallam is down in the lobby. Go report to him. He'll have fresh orders for you.'

'If Mr Hallam has more orders for me he'll come up and give 'em to me hisself,' Dunne said firmly. 'You ain't

177

getting past me tonight, mister, who-ever you are, unless Mr Hallam says it is OK. Come back in the morning.'

Hart stifled his impatience; drew his pistol fast and slammed the long barrel against Dunne's thick skull. The impact sent a shock wave up Hart's arm but had no apparent effect on Dunne, who set his right hand into motion, clawing for the butt of his gun and lifting it swiftly from its holster, his face expressing an undue eagerness to fight.

Hart struck again with his gun barrel, this time at Dunne's gun wrist as the man's weapon cleared leather. Dunne uttered a cry of pain and dropped the weapon. Hart kicked it along the corridor as he levelled his gun and jabbed the muzzle into Dunne's pro-truding stomach with a force that caused the big man to expel his breath in a painful gasp.

'Give me any trouble and you'll spend the rest of the night in jail,' Hart rapped.

Darn's left hand swept up fast, knocking aside Hart's gun. Hart lifted his knee to Dunne's groin and the big man yelped as he sagged. Hart stepped back a pace and hit Dunne across the left temple in a back-handed blow with his gun barrel. The front sight ripped flesh, and blood spurted. Dunne's big hands lifted to grasp Hart, who struck again, and this time the blow had its intended effect. Dunne fell to his knees, and then keeled over sideways; even so, he was not completely out.

Hart rapped on the door of the room and watched Dunne closely as he awaited a reply. The big man's eyelids were flickering, his breathing harsh. A key turned in the lock of the door, which opened a fraction, and Beth Straker peered out. Relief swamped her expression when she saw Hart, but she frowned at the sight of Dunne lying at the Ranger's feet.

'I heard a commotion out here,' Beth commented. 'What's going on?'

'I wanted to talk to you, and had to come through some opposition. Perhaps *you'll* tell *me* what's going on. I heard you'd had some trouble with Hallam. Why was Dunne guarding your door? Are you a prisoner in your room?'

'It seems that way, although Brent said it was for my own good because I was talking about hauling Grandfather back to the ranch in the morning.'

'How is Sam?'

'Doc Crane says he shouldn't be moved for several days yet'

'So what's happened to make you decide to go against the doctor's orders?'

'It's the same old thing. Brent is impatient to take over Double S and Grandfather isn't ready to retire yet.'

'So Hallam has tried to buy you out?'

'Yes, several times, but this time he became just too insistent, and when I told him so he lost his temper. But I expect he'll be more reasonable in the morning. It's nothing, really. Brent is worried about Grandfather and me because he knows Radd has been frequenting the spread, and now Sam is on his back it looks like we need help.'

Hart was watching Dunne while listening to Beth. When the big man got to his hands and knees, Hart covered him with his pistol.

'Stay still, Dunne. We'll go down to see Hallam together.' He returned his attention to Beth. 'I need to talk to Sam, but I won't bother him now. I'll come and see him in the morning. If the doctor says he shouldn't be moved then you'd better take notice.'

'If we do leave it won't be early in the morning. I'll have to arrange for a wagon to pick us up because Grandfather wouldn't be able to ride a saddle-horse, whatever happens.'

'I'll leave you in peace now.' Hart backed off and turned to face Dunne. 'If you do need any help during the night then just call for me, Miss Straker.'

He motioned for Dunne to precede him, and followed the big man along the corridor. He heard Beth lock her door before turning his full attention to the matter in hand. Dunne descended the stairs heavily with Hart in close attendance. Hallam was standing alone by the reception desk.

Hallam's face was hosting a scowl when he looked up and saw Hart behind the discomfited Dunne.

'Give Dunne new orders,' Hart said brusquely. 'He's not needed outside Beth Straker's room. You'd better pull in your horns about Double S, Hallam, or you'll find yourself in trouble with the law.'

'It's none of your damn business!' Hallam grated. 'You're overstepping yourself, Ranger, and I won't stand for that.'

'The jail is a mite overcrowded at the moment, but I'm sure we can squeeze in you and your hardcases.' Hart spoke softly, but there was menace in his tone.

'I would have thought you had enough to do around here without picking on honest folk in town,' Hallam retorted through his teeth. Hart was tempted to strike the hotelier, but held his hand.

'What's got you riled up?' he demanded. 'You've got your finger in a number of pies around here, huh? And the law is getting mighty close to opening up some of them, which I guess is giving you sleepless nights.'

'I don't have a notion what you are talking about,' Hallam replied.

'Why did your hardcase Mason leave town suddenly? I heard he collected a slug the other evening, and the only shots fired around town were between me and someone who took a shot at me. Send word to your spread that I wanta talk to Mason, so get him back here soon as you can, and then we'll find out just what is going on.'

Hallam did not reply. Hart studied the hotelier's set face for a moment, then departed swiftly, but paused on the sidewalk outside the street door to catch any exchange of talk between Hallam and Dunne.

'You better ride out to the spread and tell Mason to get lost for a few days in case that Ranger goes out there snooping around,' Hallam said.

'It would be easier if I put a slug in that long-nose,' Dunne replied.

'Kill a Ranger?' Hallam laughed. 'Are you crazy? You nail one of them and we'll be knee-deep in Rangers. I've got close to what I want now, and I ain't losing my nerve and tossing it all away. Do like I say and we'll play the rest of the game with our cards close to our chests. Radd is our ace in the hole. He can take the blame for anything that happens around here.'

'So that's why you've acted friendly with him. OK, let me kill the Ranger and Radd will get the credit.' Dunne laughed brutally. 'You can't lose, boss.'

'I'll think about it. Get out to the spread and warn Mason to lie low for a spell, just in case, and by the time you get back here I'll have a better idea of what to do next.'

'OK. But I don't like it. That Ranger ain't a fool, and he'll be working on what's happened here tonight. I said it was stupid having me riding herd on

Beth Straker. You pushed her too hard, and now she's got her back up you won't be able to do a thing with her.'

'Just do like you're told and leave Double S to me,' Hallam retorted.

Hart moved away from the door and paused in deeper shadows. Dunne emerged from the hotel and hurried away along the sidewalk towards the livery barn. Hart glanced around the quiet street and then set out after Dunne. The hardcase did not look left or right as he hurried to the stable, and Hart was only feet behind him when he entered the barn.

Palming his pistol, Hart slid in through the entrance and moved to one side. A lantern was alight, suspended from a nail in an overhead beam, and its beams filled the barn with heavy shadows. Dunne approached a stall on the left, and Hart closed in on him. Dunne picked up a bridle and turned to a grey horse that whinnied a greeting.

'Hold it, Dunne,' Hart called. 'You

won't need that horse. You're not going anywhere, except to jail.'

Dunne swung around, his face showing surprise. The next instant he hurled the bridle into Hart's face, and came forward with a lunging movement that brought him within an arm's length of the Ranger, his right hand clawing for his holstered pistol. Hart dropped his pistol and sledged his right fist into Dunne's stomach, his left hand sneaking out to secure a grip on Dunne's gun wrist. Dunne cleared leather before Hart could stop him, and each used brute strength to gain control of the weapon.

Hart struck again with his right fist, his bunched knuckles slamming against Dunne's solid chin. The man wrenched his pistol out of Hart's grasp and triggered the weapon as it swung up to present the gaping muzzle at Hart's body. Hart blocked the move with his left hand even as the gun exploded, and the bullet missed him by a hair's breadth. The shot hammered hollowly inside the building, and gun smoke flared.

Hart smashed his forehead into Dunne's face. The big man staggered backwards at the impact. His nose crumpled and blood spurted from his nostrils. Hart secured a hold on Dunne's pistol and twisted viciously, forcing the weapon upwards and away. The gun was fired again, its noise blasting against Hart's ear drums. Hart lifted his knee to Dunne's belly and the man staggered and tried to turn away.

Putting pressure on Dunne's hand, Hart forced it back against the wrist joint. The pistol fell to the ground. Dunne swung his left fist and his knuckles grazed Hart's chin. Hart countered with his right to the stomach, and then whirled in a left hook that caught Dunne's right eye. Dunne moved back, shaking his head, and Hart gave him no respite, following closely, throwing punches that slammed into Dunne's body.

Dunne began to run out of steam.

He backed off, lifting his hands defensively, and Hart tore into him, his big fists working like sledge-hammers. He threw a flurry of punches to Dunne's head, switched to the body and had Dunne gasping in distress before delivering a right to the jaw that sent the man pitching to the ground. Dunne landed on his back, made an effort to rise, and then slumped back, his hands unclenching. He lay gasping for breath, his mouth agape and his eyes closed.

Hart rubbed his knuckles and then picked up his pistol. He stuck the weapon into its holster and bent over Dunne, grasping the man's thick shoulder and pulling him upright. Dunne staggered, shaking his head.

'You know where the jail is,' Hart told him. 'Let's have no more trouble, huh? I like a quiet life.'

Dunne staggered to the door and they went along the street. Hart stayed back out of reach, his right hand close to his gun butt. They passed the hotel, and then the saloon. Hart glanced into the lobby of the hotel as they passed, and saw it was deserted.

Frank Burnside was drinking coffee when Dunne pushed open the law office door and entered. Hart followed closely and closed the door with a spurred boot. Two townsmen were lounging on chairs near the desk; they straightened up at the sight of Dunne.

'Trouble?' Burnside asked, noting Hart's bruised face.

'Nothing I couldn't handle,' Hart replied. 'Have we got room for one more in the cells?'

'There's plenty of room! What's the charge against Dunne?'

'Resisting arrest will do until I find out more about Hallam's activities. I need to pick up Mason, who's out at Hallam's ranch. If he did shoot at me from cover the other evening then we're in business in a big way. I've got a line on Hallam's interests, and there's no telling where an investigation might lead.'

'I'm about to make a round of the

town,' Burnside said, after putting Dunne in a cell. 'Saturday night is always busy with the cattle outfits in for some weekend fun. I'll keep an eye open for Mason. He might have come in with the rest of Hallam's bunch.'

'I need to get a meal,' Hart mused, 'and then I'll start questioning the prisoners. I want to know why Radd went off to Cottonwood Creek, how Santee knew where to join him, and why Radd got Santee to bring Cindy Harmon to San Fedora.'

'I asked a few question earlier but no one was talking.' Burnside hitched up his sagging gunbelt. 'You might have better luck than me.'

The deputy departed and Hart turned to the two townsmen.

'I hope you're both on your toes,' he said. 'Radd might be badly wounded, but he'll be out of here if you give him half a chance.'

'We're ready for anything,' one of them replied. 'No one is gonna get away from us.'

'Keep the street-door locked, and check the identity of anyone wanting to come in.' Hart went to the door leading to the cells and opened it.

A lamp was burning in the cell block, casting dim light through the cells. Hart walked along the corridor, looking into the cells. Radd was huddled in a blanket on his bunk, either asleep or unconscious, as was Santee in the next cell. Ike Gotch was seated on the foot of his bunk, and did not look up as Hart inspected him through the bars.

'Not looking so good right now, huh, Gotch?' Hart commented. The outlaw looked up but made no reply.

Hart continued his inspection, and then returned to the office. The two jailers were checking their pistols, and one of them got up to lock the street door when Hart departed. The town was quiet, Hart noted, and he went to a restaurant for a meal. The big room was packed but he found a vacant table and sat down. He was about through eating when several shots rang out. He was on his feet and hurrying to the door before those around him had recovered from their surprise.

Gun echoes were still sounding across the town when Hart paused on the sidewalk, gun in hand. Men were spilling out of the saloon to stand in a group on the sidewalk, looking around. A man came along the street at a run, and Hart called to him as he approached.

'What's the trouble?' Hart demanded.

'Frank Burnside has been shot. I saw it happen. He was going into the stable when two men opened up on him. I'm fetching the doc, but I don't think Burnside is alive.'

Hart set off at a run for the stable, hoping against hope that the report was wrong.

9

The livery barn was in total darkness when Hart reached it. He paused in deep shadow and looked around, sensing that the two men who had been seen attacking the deputy had gone. He edged into the barn, holstered his gun and struck a match, his muscles tensed in anticipation of a shot, but nothing happened. He lifted down the lamp and relit it. His gaze fell immediately upon the inert body of Frank Burnside lying just inside the doorway.

Blood stained the front of the deputy's shirt. Hart dropped to one knee beside the figure, and was relieved to find signs of life. Burnside's heart was beating faintly. Burnside opened his eyes. Blood was trickling from a corner of his mouth. He looked ghastly in the dim lantern-light.

'Take it easy, Frank,' Hart said. 'The

doc is on his way. Did you see the men who shot you?'

'Two men were waiting in here and they surprised me. Hallam's hardcase, Mason, was one of them, and Chuck Fenn, Hallam's ranch foreman, was the other. Mason's left arm was bandaged — it looks like he was the one you shot the other night. He gunned me down without giving me a chance — him and Fenn. Get 'em for me, Hart.'

'You can bet on that,' Hart responded.

Burnside heaved a long sigh and lapsed into unconsciousness. Hart waited stolidly until he heard footsteps approaching the barn, then Doc Crane appeared, carrying his bag. The doctor dropped to his knees beside the deputy. After a cursory examination he looked up at Hart, then grimaced and shook his head.

'He ain't got too many chances of making it,' Crane said. 'I reckon all I can do is make him comfortable. Do you know who shot him?'

'He told me.' Hart left the barn and

went back along the street grappling with his emotions. He turned into the hotel and confronted the receptionist.

'Is Hallam here?' he demanded.

'No,' she replied. 'He left some time ago. I believe he was going to the saloon to have a drink with his ranch crew. It's a regular thing on a Saturday night.'

'Thanks.' Hart departed and went on to the saloon.

He peered in over the batwings, his eyes narrowed as he sought the figure of the hotelier. There were close to thirty men in the big room. Cigarette-smoke was thick, and a great hum of voices, talking and laughing, filled the smoky atmosphere. There was no sign of Hallam.

Hart pushed through the batwings and left them swinging at his back. No one took any notice of him. He did not know any of Hallam's ranch crew by sight, and approached an old man standing at the near corner of the bar.

'Take a look around and tell me if you see any of Brent Hallam's ranch crew in here,' Hart said.

'I don't need to look around. Hallam came in about twenty minutes ago and had a chat with his foreman, Chuck Fenn. When they left they took their crew with them.'

'Thanks.' Hart went outside and stood on the sidewalk, looking around.

The town was quiet, away from the saloon. The street was practically deserted. Hart glanced towards the law office. All was peaceful. He glanced in the opposite direction and saw a group of figures emerging from the livery barn. Frank Burnside was being carried on a door, the figure of the doctor, easily recognizable, hurrying along behind. Hart shook his head, drew a long breath, and held it for several moments before releasing it in a long sigh. He came to a sudden decision and walked towards the law office, sensing that the town was too quiet for a Saturday night. He was impatient for action.

He reached the alley that ran

alongside the jail. As he crossed its dark mouth a figure loomed up out of its shadows and a hand snatched his pistol from its holster. Hart whirled instantly sensing rather than seeing an uplifted hand gripping a pistol descending towards his head. He tried to duck away, felt his hat being pulled from his head, and then received a blow on his skull that caused a fiery explosion in his brain. He had no sense of pain. Blackness burst behind his eyes. He was dimly aware of falling and then all sight and sound were blotted out as he plunged into a bottomless pit that engulfed everything . . .

★   ★   ★

Pain dragged Hart back to consciousness, a nagging, throbbing headache, and for an interminable time he lay blinking in total darkness, trying to regain his scattered wits. His hands were bound, his senses informed him. He was lying on his back and being jolted interminably — covered with a blanket that reached above his eyes so that he could not look around.

The sound of wheels grating on hard ground indicated that he was stretched out on the hard bed of a wagon. He was obsessed by the pain in his head, and had no idea how much time had passed since he was attacked, but cramp was seeping into his hands and he tried to ease his position. There was a sharp pain in his lower back on the left, and he realized that it was caused by the small .41 derringer in the back pocket of his pants. He struggled to loosen the bonds around his wrists but realized it was useless; then he lay helpless, his body rolling with the motion of the wagon.

The pain in his head lessened as time passed, but the incessant jolting of the wagon sickened him. He tried to work the covering blanket down from his eyes, but his hands were useless. He wondered where he was being taken, and presently heard the sound of approaching hoofs. Voices sounded and he lay very still, listening intently. He recognized Brent Hallam's harsh tone.

'Is that Ranger alive, Chuck?' Hallam demanded.

'Hell if I know. Smith gave him a dent in his skull in that alley, and I ain't heard a squeak outa him since we slung him in the wagon. His hands are tied so it don't matter if he's dead or alive. We'll finish him off at the ranch, and bury him in an unmarked grave so no one will find him. That should take care of the Rangers. If they come nosing around you can put the blame on Radd. It was a good idea springing him outa jail. The heat will be on him, and he can be blamed for everything that happens around here.'

'That's why I busted him out.' Hallam chuckled.

'You're a fool if you think you can get away with what you're trying,' a woman's voice cut in.

Hart frowned as he recognized Beth Straker's voice. She was obviously in the wagon, and only inches from him.

'Are you going to kill Grandfather and me as well?' Beth demanded. 'You'll have to if you want to keep your crooked plan secret. You won't get your hands on Double S any other way. Grandfather would rather die than sign the ranch over to you, you cheap crook, and I won't keep quiet about you after this.'

'I'm sorry this has turned out the way it has, Beth,' Hallam replied smoothly. 'You can thank the Ranger, for sticking his long nose into my business. I wanted to do this the nice way, but I'm gonna have to put you and Sam out of it now — it's the only way, and we could have had a good life together.'

'Huh!' Scorn sounded in Beth Straker's tone. 'How long do you suppose you could have fooled me? I was getting wise to your motives, anyway.'

'It could have worked,' Hallam insisted. 'Now I'll have to figure out another solution, and it looks like it'll have to be done the hard way. Hurry up and get this wagon to the ranch, Chuck. I'll ride on ahead.'

The clatter of departing hoofs indicated that Hallam had ridden on. Hart was shocked by what he had heard. Buck Radd had been turned loose again, and although badly wounded, the outlaw would soon begin fresh depredations. He began to work on his bonds again, but with little success. The wagon was heading for Hallam's ranch, and he needed to be free before they reached it if he were have any chance of escaping this grim situation.

The blanket was suddenly tweaked from Hart's body and he lifted his head to look around. Starlight was filtering down through the blackness of the night, and a slender crescent of the moon showed high in the west, sailing serenely through the velvet sky. A small oval face showed indistinctly almost beside Hart, and he vaguely recognized Beth Straker, who saw his slight movement and lifted a finger to her lips.

The girl was sitting beside the inert figure of Sam Straker.

Hart relaxed and lay still. The next instant the girl reached over him, located his bound wrists, and began to work on the rope binding him. Minutes passed before her efforts succeeded and he felt the rope loosen. When it fell away, he suffered untold agonies as his restricted circulation began to flow normally. He clenched his teeth, flexed his fingers, and eventually normal feelings came back into his hands.

Hart craned his neck and looked up over his head to see the dark figure of the man who was driving the wagon; at the same time he reached awkwardly for the derringer in his back pocket. His fingers closed around the small weapon and he lifted it carefully as he eased himself unsteadily up on one knee. He stuck the muzzle of the gun against the nape of the driver's neck, and felt the man's sudden stiffening of his muscles.

'Just sit still, mister,' Hart grated, 'and maybe you might live to see the sun when it comes up.'

He transferred the derringer to his left hand and snatched the pistol from the man's holster; the noise of it, as he cocked the weapon, sounded most pleasant. Pain was still throbbing in his head but was tolerable now. Hart blinked as he looked around. There were no accompanying riders, and a saddle-horse was tied to the back of the wagon.

'Stop the wagon and throw up your hands,' Hart ordered. The man obeyed.

'Let me drive and we'll head for Double S,' Beth cut in. 'I want to get Grandfather to bed as soon as possible, and our crew will soon handle Hallam and his outfit when I tell them what's happened.'

'How far to Double S from here?' Hart demanded.

Beth looked around to get her bearings. 'About eight miles.'

'Will your outfit be on the spread? Won't everyone be in town?'

'It's after midnight now. I reckon the

boys will be in their bunks on the ranch at this hour.'

'OK, so you drive on to Double S.' Hart decided. 'I'll tie this galoot's hands and you can take him with you. Keep him prisoner until I can get back to you. I think he's one of the men who shot Frank Burnside.'

'What are you gonna do?' Beth asked. 'It will be better for you to have some of our crew along if you're going after Hallam.'

'I heard Hallam say he'd turned my prisoners loose in town, and I want him for that. I'll pick him up at his place and drop by Double S on my way back to San Fedora. I need to get on Buck Radd's trail soon as I can. That crook won't be able to move fast, the condition he's in, and I want him back behind bars before he can start operating again. He won't let his wounds tie him down. He'll soon have his outfit out raiding.'

Beth tied the driver's hands while Hart held a gun on the man. Then Hart untied the horse tethered to the back of the wagon. He swung into the saddle and rode in beside Beth, who had climbed into the driving-seat of the vehicle.

'How do I get to Hallam's spread from here?' he asked.

'The trail we're on will lead you right into Hallam's yard. Please do as I say and get some help behind you.'

'I can't afford to waste time.' Hart shook his head. 'Hallam won't be expecting me so I should be able to pick him up with no trouble. You'll be all right now. I'll see you later.'

The girl nodded and whipped the team. The wagon started forward and swung away from the trail under the girl's expert driving. Hart watched its progress for some minutes as it headed for the distant Double S. When it had vanished into the gloom he touched spurs to the saddle-horse and set off along the faint trail towards Brent Hallam's ranch.

Hart rode steadily. His head was

aching dully, and his forehead was stiff with dried blood. He was hatless, and felt far from his usual self. His thoughts were restless. His successful second hunt for Buck Radd had been in vain, for the outlaw was on the loose again, and the task of recapturing him lay before Hart like an insurmountable barrier.

The horse Hart was riding was accustomed to the trail to Hallam's spread, and cantered willingly. Hart gave the animal its head and was halfway down a slope when he picked up the sound of approaching hoofs. Caught out in the open, there was nowhere he could ride into cover, and he decided to keep riding as if he had a right to be heading for Hallam's ranch.

Two riders loomed up out of the night. They were travelling fast, and Hart reined in as they parted to avoid running him down. He heard a shout of surprise, and then both men were reining in. They swept by Hart and swung to come back to him. He covered them with the gun in his hand.

'Who are you?' one of them challenged as they halted a couple of yards from Hart.

'It's the Ranger!' the other ejaculated.

'That's right,' Hart replied. 'Throw up your hands.'

His words triggered both men into violent action. The one on Hart's left dived from his saddle while the other reached for his holstered gun. Hart caught the glint of starlight on a lifting weapon and fired instantly, the big pistol bucking hard against the heel of his hand. The man on the right fell over back-wards out of his saddle, but his left foot became trapped in a stirrup and he was dragged violently as the horse whirled away from the shooting.

Hart dismounted, putting the horse between himself and the other man. For a moment Hart was unable to see the man, but then he came surging to his feet, pistol lifting. Shaking his head, Hart lifted his thumb from the hammer of the gun and the weapon flamed and blasted. The bullet took the man in the centre of the chest and he fell inertly, dead before he hit the ground. Hart stood motionless with uplifted pistol while the harsh echoes of the shooting rolled away across the darkened range.

When full silence returned, Hart checked out the two men. Both were dead, and he wondered what kind of a desperate errand they had been on that warranted fighting to the death. He returned to his horse and remounted to carry on, aware that the smell of gun smoke and death travelled with him.

Hart spotted lights on the range a long time before he reached Hallam's spread. He reined in a couple of hundred yards from the ranch. He reloaded his pistol before moving in on foot, and was crossing the yard when he was challenged from the shadows around the corral on his left.

'Hands up and declare yourself,' a harsh voice commanded.

Hart stopped in mid-stride, turning

to face the figure that came forward out of the gloom. He saw a man carrying a Winchester, which was pointing directly at him, and raised his hands obediently.

'Don't you know it's dangerous to walk into a yard after dark?' the guard demanded.

'I need a horse,' Hart said. 'Mine broke a leg in a gopher hole. I was making for San Fedora, saw your lights, and reckoned to pick up a remount to finish my trip.'

'You've come to the wrong place for help,' the man replied. He halted in front of Hart, his rifle levelled waist high. 'Callers ain't welcome any time. We'll go talk to the boss, but I warn you, he ain't in a good mood right now.'

'All I want is to borrow a horse,' Hart said.

'Head for the house.' The guard chuckled. 'I'd like to hear how Hallam reacts to you.'

Hart walked on to the house and paused when he reached the porch. When the guard jabbed him with the muzzle of the rifle he spun around and side-stepped, his hands lifting to wrench the rifle out of the guard's grasp. He slammed the butt against the man's jaw, and then reversed the weapon, but it was not needed for the man fell limply to the ground and rolled inertly.

'That was neatly done,' a voice observed from the deep shadows at the back of the porch. 'Don't do anything except breathe, mister. I got a gun pointed at your middle. Drop the rifle and get your hands up. Who are you and what are you doing prowling around here on foot?'

Hart was relieved that the unknown man was not Brent Hallam. He dropped the rifle and raised his hands. Yellow lamplight was issuing from a window of the house to the right, but it did not reveal any details of the man. Hart repeated his story about his horse breaking a leg.

'OK, so come ahead and enter the house. Move slow and we'll talk to the boss. Be careful not to make a fast move because I'm real nervous, and I'll start shooting if I think you're gonna try something smart.'

'You're real cautious around here,' Hart observed.

'Orders from the boss. He rode in some time ago and put us on alert. I don't know what is going on yet, but we're all loaded for bear. It's too bad you had to show up at this particular time.'

Hart crossed the porch and opened the door of the house. He felt his pistol being removed from its holster as he passed the man. There was bright light in the big living-room into which he walked, and he saw Brent Hallam seated at a roll-top desk, busy with ranch paper-work. Hallam looked up at Hart's entrance, recognized the Ranger, and sprang to his feet with an oath, his usually smooth gambler's face contorted by shock.

'What the hell are you doing here?' he demanded. 'What's happened to Beth and Sam? Is the wagon outside? I didn't hear it crossing the yard.'

Hart lowered his hands, mindful of the fact that his .41 derringer was nestling in his back right-hand pocket.

'Beth is driving the wagon to Double S,' Hart said. 'I doubt you'll want to ride in there when she has alerted their outfit. In fact, I expect that her crew will wanta ride in here to take up matters with you. I can save you a lot of grief by arresting you and taking you back to San Fedora.'

'You ain't goin' anywhere,' Hallam grated. 'You'll be dead by sun-up. Watch out for him, Payne. He's a Ranger and good at his job. He's arrested Buck Radd twice. I had to bust Radd loose from the jail before I came on to the ranch.'

'And that's why I wanta arrest you,' Hart said flatly.

'You better stand still, keep quiet, and stay cool, mister,' Payne rasped. 'I ain't bothered by the thought of killing a Ranger. I'll take him out right now and drop him, if you give the word, boss.'

Hart glanced over his shoulder at the gunman. At that moment the door was thrust open and the guard staggered in from the porch, his rifle in his hand. Payne glanced towards the door. Hart clenched his teeth and swept into action. He reached into his back pocket and his hand reappeared holding the two-shot derringer. Payne was bringing his attention back to Hart, saw the danger and brought up his gun hand. Hart fired, saw dust fly from Payne's shirt front, and covered the still-dazed guard, who dropped his rifle.

Moving swiftly, Hart positioned himself where he could cover Hallam and the guard. Hallam had reached for his holstered pistol, but stilled the movement when Hart's deadly hideout gun turned its black eye towards him.

'That's better,' Hart remarked, grasping the guard by a shoulder and thrusting him towards the motionless Hallam. Hart followed him closely and snaked Hallam's gun from leather. He cocked the weapon, returned his derringer to its pocket and jabbed Hallam in the stomach with the muzzle of the pistol. 'I don't want any more trouble from you,' he warned the hotelier. 'Stay quiet and do like I say or you'll feel the full weight of the law coming down on you. So you turned my prisoners loose from the jail, and no doubt gave orders for Frank Burnside to be shot down.'

'You can't pin anything on me,' Hallam retorted. 'And if you think you can get away from here then you better think again. I've got my crew on guard, and they let you come into the spread, but they won't let you out again. You've come to the end of your trail, Ranger.'

As if to vindicate the warning, a voice called from the porch.

'We got the place surrounded so you better come on out with your hands up.'

Hart grinned. He jabbed his gun muzzle against Hallam's spine.

'You'll get it first if shooting starts,' he warned. 'Better call off your wolves,

Hallam. I don't quit on a job. It's always a fight to the finish for me, and I'm holding all the high cards. You were a gambler once, so let's see you play your way out of this situation.'

A pane of glass in the window at the far end of the room suddenly splintered and tinkled. Hart moved in behind Hallam, and the next instant the big room was filled with gunsmoke and flying lead. Hart put a shot into the lamp on the desk, and ducked as darkness swept in, aware that the hunting and searching for the bad men was over. This was clean-up time.

10

Hallam did not move as the lamp was extinguished, for the muzzle of Hart's pistol was jammed against his spine. Hart tripped the hotelier and went down to the floor with him. He struck hard with his gun, slamming the barrel against Hallam's head, and heard a groan as the man slumped into unconsciousness. Gun-flashes split the darkness of the room, and hot lead flailed through the air. Hart remained low, waiting for the lethal storm to abate. Two guns were firing into the room from different windows. Hart's left hand rested on Hallam's shoulder.

The shooting lessened slowly, then dwindled away. Hart waited, aware that the initiative was not his. A harsh voice called out from outside the window at the end of the room.

'You better give up now and come

out with your hands high,' the voice directed.

'No. I got a better idea,' Hart replied. 'Hallam is unconscious in here and under my gun, so you get the hell out with the rest of the bunch and I'll mosey back to town with Hallam as my prisoner. He's finished in this county now, and any of his outfit still around after I've jailed him will be next in line for trouble from the law.'

There was no reply. The ensuing silence stretched on and on interminably. Hart checked Hallam, who was still unconscious, then got to his feet and eased towards the door. He heard the sound of hoofs departing in the background as he opened the door and stepped out on to the porch. He wondered if his threat had worked. Was Hallam's crew making a run for it?

Standing in the thick shadows on the porch, Hart looked around for trouble. He moved to his left and a loose board creaked under his boot. He froze, but there was no reaction from the surrounding night. His ears were strained for hostile sounds, but he began to hope that his threat had worked. It was on the cards that the gunslingers would pull out if their wages had stopped.

Moving slowly, Hart made a complete circuit of the house, and discovered that the gunmen had pulled out, although he suspected that they would be lying in wait for him somewhere along the trail to town. He went back into the house and struck a match. A lamp was standing on a long table and he lit it before checking Hallam. The man was beginning to stir, and Hart waited patiently until Hallam's eyes opened.

'You're under arrest,' Hart said crisply. 'We'll be heading back to town shortly.'

'My outfit won't let you get away with it,' Hallam responded, feeling his head gingerly. 'You're dead the minute you stick your nose outside that door.'

'I've already been outside.' Hart

grinned. 'Your men have pulled out. They know you're beaten and they ain't sticking around to face the music. You're on your own now, Hallam, and I'm taking you in.'

'You won't get far,' Hallam sneered.

'Far enough to jail you,' Hart promised.

Hallam did not reply, and Hart searched around the big room for a rope. Hallam made no attempt at resistance as he was bound, and Hart led him to the back door of the house. They stood in deep shadow while Hart checked his surroundings. When he was satisfied they were alone, he led the hotelier across to the barn.

Hart was at the top of his alertness. He carried his pistol in his right hand, ready-cocked for trouble, but the night breeze blew gently around him and he sensed that they were alone. He tied Hallam to a post inside the barn.

'You make one sound while I'm saddling a horse for you and I'll gut-shoot you,' Hart warned.

He was ready for trouble as he took a

horse from the nearby corral, led it into the barn and saddled it. When he was ready to move out he hoisted Hallam into the saddle and tied him there, all without a sound coming from any other part of the ranch headquarters. He set off in a wide circle from behind the corral, leading Hallam's horse as he made for the spot where he had left his own mount. Nothing stirred around him.

His horse whickered as he neared it, and Hart tied the reins of Hallam's mount to a tree and prepared to fetch his own animal. He expected a gun trap, and inched forward to where his animal was waiting, skirting the area first in a circle that revealed nothing; then quickly he collected the horse and returned for Hallam. He was relieved when they were moving out of the immediate area.

It was Hart's intention to ride back to San Fedora and jail Hallam, but he was worried about Beth Straker and swung east to locate the Double S. Two miles along the trail gun-flame split the darkness ahead and he heard the crackle of a bullet passing over his head. He dismounted quickly, dragged Hallam out of his saddle, and lay listening to the fading echoes, his pistol in his hand.

Full silence returned, and then a voice called from the shadows.

'Ranger, turn Hallam loose and we'll let you go.'

Hart grinned, but made no reply. He waited while the silence continued, and then arose, pushed Hallam back into his saddle, and continued. The moon had passed beyond the peak of a mountain to the west and shadows were thicker now. Hart rode at a walk, with Hallam's tied reins over his saddle horn.

Twice more, shots were fired at Hart from the surrounding shadows. After the second time Hallam cursed because a speeding bullet missed him by a hair's breadth.

'Lay off, will you?' he yelled. 'You nearly hit me. Wait until you can draw a bead on the Ranger.'

'OK, boss,' a harsh voice replied. 'We'll hang back till dawn. See you when the sun comes up.'

Hart decided to camp until dawn, and loosened cinches. He ground-hobbled the horses, then settled down beside Hallam, his gun in hand. He was tired but gave no thought to sleeping, and whiled away the time by thinking over the situation.

The blackness of night was turning slowly to grey when Hart arose and sneaked away into the shadows to check out his surroundings. He circled the two horses and the hotelier, moving outwards carefully, looking for the rest of Hallam's crew. Fifty yards out from his camp, he heard a horse whinny, and dropped into cover, his gun cocked.

The sound did not come again, and Hart began to crawl forward. He covered twenty yards before hearing the mumble of voices, and then paused to listen.

'I reckon we're making a big mistake,

Al,' someone was saying. 'That's a Ranger with the boss, and I learned at an early age not to mix it with them guys. Hallam is finished, and if we got any sense we'll fade from here and make for greener pastures.'

'There's still a lot of money to be made around here,' Al replied. 'If the Ranger is killed then Radd will get the blame, so we can't lose. I'm gonna get that Ranger soon as the sun comes up.'

'Well, I been thinking, and I don't want anything to do with it,' the other said. 'I'm gonna haul my freight. Hallam is on a losing run, trying to take over Straker's spread. That old man was a Ranger hisself years ago, and Hallam can't buck that situation nohow. I'm leaving.'

'You're free to go,' Al sneered. 'Me, I'm sticking. I ain't no piker. I reckon Hallam will come out on top.'

Hart waited patiently. The darkness of night receded imperceptibly. He heard the sudden beat of hoofs on hard ground as a rider departed. He began to move forward again. Presently he made out the shape of a horse standing head down, and caught the pungent smell of cigarette-smoke as he moved in like a prowling wolf.

A man got up suddenly and began to roll his blankets. Hart covered him with his pistol, and then spoke:

'I got you covered,' he called. 'Throw your hands up and keep 'em there.'

The man froze, then slowly raised his hands shoulder high. Hart stood up and moved in. He jabbed his muzzle against the man's spine and relieved him of a pistol. The man did not attempt to resist. Hart stepped back and looked around.

'Your sidekick showed more sense,' Hart observed. 'He knew when it was time to pull out. You can ride with your boss to town and try the jail for a spell.'

The man did not reply. Hart bound him, helped him into his saddle, and then led the animal back to his own camp, where Hallam was waiting stolidly. Within minutes Hart broke camp and led the way east, making for Double S in the growing light of day.

Full daylight came, and Hart saw a wagon approaching from the east with two riders in attendance. As the vehicle drew nearer, he recognized Beth Straker driving. The girl stopped the wagon and picked up a Winchester when she saw Hart, covering him as he closed the distance between them. The two cowboys watched him with hands on their holstered guns and suspicion in their eyes until Beth spoke to them, when they relaxed visibly.

'Last night you were going to Double S,' Hart said, reining in by the wagon.

'I played it cagey when I got there.' Beth was grim-faced. 'And it's a good thing I did. I left the wagon out of range and went in on foot to check the spread. Radd was there with most of his gang and Bull Santee and his two sidekicks. They'd made themselves at home, and looked like they were planning on a long stay. I sneaked away again, picked up Mike and Bill, and came in this direction to warn you because I knew you were headed out to the BH spread.' She paused and looked at Hart's two prisoners. 'So you got Hallam, huh? It's a pity you didn't shoot him.'

Hart grinned. 'I would have done if he'd given me reason to. Why don't you turn this rig around and head back to town? How is Sam this morning?'

'Not very good. He should never have left his bed in San Fedora. If anything happens to him because he was put in this wagon last night I'll take a gun to Hallam myself.'

Hart looked in the wagon. Sam Straker was lying on a pile of straw, asleep or unconscious. He was pale-faced, exhausted, and breathing heavily. Hallam's ranch foreman, who had driven the wagon the night before, was lying on his back beside Sam, his wrists and ankles bound.

'You'd better turn around and head back to town,' Hart said, 'and it will help me a great deal if you'll take my two prisoners with you and lock them in the jail when you get there.'

'We can handle them.' Beth eyed Hallam with venom in her tone and hatred in her eyes. 'What are you going to do?'

'I'll mosey over to your place and do what I came here for in the first place. I want Radd and his gang, and Santee has another date with the jail in town.'

'You'll go in there alone, against half a dozen tough outlaws?' Surprise sounded in Beth's voice, and she shook her head doubtfully.

'Sure. It's expected of me, and there's only one gang, isn't there?' Hart shrugged.

'We'll take your prisoners with us,' Beth agreed.

Hart stood by while the two cowboys took charge of Hallam and his sidekick. When Beth turned the wagon and set off in the direction of town he rode east at a fast clip, following the wagon tracks from Double S and hoping against hope that Buck Radd and his men would still be at the ranch when he arrived.

It was nearing high noon when Hart topped a rise and saw the Double S ranch before him. He reined in and studied the yard, spotted a shadow at one corner of the barn and narrowed his eyes until he could make out the figure of a man holding a rifle standing beyond the corner. A trickle of emotion touched him and he drew a long breath as he pulled back off the ridge until only his head was above cover.

The man emerged from the corner and walked slowly across the yard towards the house. Hart studied the lay-out and spotted a man sitting in the shade on the porch of the house, a Winchester across his knees. He recognized Ike Gotch, and satisfaction filled him. The Radd gang was still here. He could almost smell gunsmoke, and it was no longer the product of wishful thinking now that he was in a position to attack the elusive gang.

Hart moved back down the slope and

dismounted. His mind was ticking like a clock as he considered the situation and worked out how he would handle this chore. He was outnumbered by about eight to one, but the odds did not bother him. He would go down there into the ranch, get among them, and take them as they came. He would be like a wolf among a flock of sheep, and was confident that he could handle the grim task of shooting the gang out of existence. His fingers itched to be at the show-down, but he contained his impatience.

He cleaned his pistol as he went over details in his mind. Twice before he had captured Radd only to have the man escape, but he was being offered a third chance, which he did not mean to waste. Radd did not know it yet but he had reached the end of a long trail. Hart finished his preparations, checked his cartridge-belt, and reloaded empty loops from a box of .45 cartridges he took from his saddle-bag.

He left the horse standing with

trailing reins and used the lie of the range to cover his approach to the ranch, walking in a circle to get behind the barn, which he did without incident. There was a back door to the barn. He entered the low, gloomy building and made his way to the front door, where he found a knot-hole through which to observe the yard.

Ike Gotch was still on the porch but there was no sign of the guard. Hart watched patiently, aware that his best course was to take these men separately, if possible, but there looked to be little chance of that. He went back to the rear door and stepped outside, then began a circuitous walk to the rear of the ranch house, gun in hand and his alertness at top notch.

The silence was brooding, heavy, and nothing moved except a dozen chickens scratching in the thick dust. Hart looked around, ready to fight or drop into cover, but he gained the rear of the house without incident, and was faintly surprised by his success. Radd must be feeling secure here, with Sam Straker and Beth supposedly under guard by Hallam's outfit.

Hart moved to the back door of the house. He had to pass a window to reach the door. He paused to peer into the big kitchen. He ducked back instantly. Bull Santee was inside, evidently preparing a meal. Hart ducked below the sill and continued, feeling as if he had struck gold. He tried the back door with his left hand and it opened noiselessly. He stepped into the kitchen and levelled his pistol at the renegade deputy sheriff, who was so intent on what he was doing that he failed to notice Hart's menacing figure. Santee was making a noon meal, working one-handed and awkwardly.

'Throw your hands up, Santee,' Hart said softly. 'One sound out of you and you're dead.'

Santee's head jerked around on his thick neck and he stiffened at the sight of Hart, his eyes filling with surprise.

'Where in hell did you come from?'

he snarled. 'Hallam said he'd got you. He reckoned you'd be dead at sun-up and buried before noon.'

'Hallam got it wrong.' Hart grinned. 'I always suspected you of being a bad 'un, Santee. Now you've come to the end of your trail. Get rid of your gun, and do it slow.'

Santee's face showed defiance. He reached for his pistol, using forefinger and thumb, and slowly drew the weapon from its holster. He paused then, glaring at Hart as he considered the odds.

'I don't figure to give in,' he rasped. 'Let's start over. I'll holster the gun and then we'll go to it, huh?'

'You reckon you can beat me?' Hart shook his head. 'Some other time, perhaps. I wanta get the drop on Radd and his bunch and a shot now will bring them out shooting. Drop the gun, Santee, and take your medicine.'

Santee hesitated for a split second, and then flipped up the pistol and made a desperate effort to grasp the butt and work the hammer. Hart lifted his thumb from his hammer and the weapon blasted like the crack of doom. Gun smoke flared and Santee fell back a pace under the impact of a slug of lead. A red splotch appeared as if by magic in the centre of his massive chest. He tripped over his own feet and went sprawling backwards, still trying to work his pistol, and such was his desperation that he managed to force the muzzle in Hart's direction.

Hart paused, and when Santee's gun was almost lined up on him he sent a second shot into the crooked deputy's chest. Santee relaxed, his heels drumming on the hard floor. Hart grimaced at the pungent taste of burned powder against his teeth and turned swiftly, his ears ringing from the crash of shots, wanting to get into action before the gang could react to the shooting.

He went out of the kitchen into a passage, and ran forward silently to thrust open a door that led into the front of the house. Ben Gatting and Cal

Wenn, the two men who had ridden into town a few days earlier with Santee, were in the act of rising from a big table and reaching for their holstered guns. They hesitated at the sight of Hart and then plunged into action. Gatting dropped to one knee and cocked his pistol while Wenn threw himself sideways to the floor, gun lifting swiftly.

Hart triggered his pistol, following Wenn's movement, and saw blood spurt from the man's throat as a big .45 slug tore through flesh. Gatting fired a shot before he was lined up on Hart and the bullet crackled past Hart's left ear. Hart crouched and worked his gun, his muzzle moving to cover the man. He sent two quick shots into Gatting, his breathing restrained against flaring gunsmoke.

Echoes hammered through the house. Hart moved quickly, aware that Ike Gotch was outside. He made for the door, and was three paces from it when it was thrust open and Gotch appeared, gun in hand. Gotch had to pause to check the identity of Hart, who fired without hesitation. Gotch took the bullet in his chest and spun away, falling to the floor in a slackness of muscles that proclaimed instant death.

Hart turned and ran back into the passage, wanting to clear the ground floor of resistance. He kicked open a door on the right and peered into an office, which was empty. Boots sounded on the wooden floor over his head, and then feet were pounding down the stairs as men came to investigate the shooting. Two men were intent on joining the fight, and Hart recognized the foremost as Dunne, one of Hallam's hardcases. He wondered what the man was doing here with Radd's gang, and started shooting.

Dunne opened fire from half-way up the stairs and his bullet smacked into Hart's left arm just above the elbow. Hart clenched his teeth as pain flared through the limb but did not hesitate. His gun blasted, muzzle tilted, and

Dunne stopped abruptly, as if he had run into a wall. His knees bent and he pitched forward head first down the stairs.

The second man on the stairs sent two shots at Hart, and missed both times in his haste. Hart leaned against a wall for support and snapped a shot upwards which caught the man in the body and brought him down in a whirl of arms and legs. Echoes fled through the house. Hart recalled that there was a guard outside, but he wanted to get a sight of Radd and started up the stairs, reloading his pistol as he ascended.

A figure appeared suddenly at the top of the stairs, emerging from a bedroom on the left; it was silhouetted blackly against a tall window on the landing. He was holding a rifle, and swung the muzzle to cover Hart, who triggered his Colt, shaking the house with more gun thunder. Two bullets struck the man and he twisted to the floor, his rifle sending a shot harmlessly into the ceiling.

Hart stepped over the sprawled figure and kicked open the door on the left. The room was deserted. He turned to the right, moved in on the door there, and grasped the handle, throwing the door open with considerable force. He peered into the room and saw Radd lying in a big bed. There were two men in the room with the gang boss, and both started shooting instantly.

A bullet struck the doorpost beside Hart's head and splinters flew from the soft wood. Hart dropped to one knee, only partialy covered by the doorpost, and he could feel pain in his face where he had been struck by splinters. His gun was thrust forward, and he sent a slug into the left shoulder of the only target he could see. The man dropped his pistol and ducked out of sight behind the bed.

Radd lifted a shotgun and lined it up on the doorway. Hart ducked away as the fearsome weapon exploded, throwing himself flat as a whirling load of buckshot blew a big hole in the door.

The house shook to the blast. Hart rolled on the floor, cocking his pistol as he did so. The third man in the room came out through the doorway with his gun hammering and Hart shot him dead centre. The man pitched over and fell almost on top of Hart, but he was dead before he hit the floor.

Hart pushed the body off his legs and got to his feet. In the lull that followed he moved back to the door, staying back respectfully.

'Hey, Radd,' he called. 'Throw down that gun and surrender. You don't have to die here and now.'

'You ain't taking me alive, Ranger,' Radd replied quickly. 'Stick your nose around the doorpost and I'll decorate your face for you. If you want me then come and get me. You're gonna have to do it the hard way.'

Hart checked his pistol. His ears were ringing uncomfortably from the racket of the guns. He thrust his gun hand around the doorpost and sent two quick shots in the direction of the bed.

Radd fired both barrels of the shotgun, shredding the doorpost. Hart stepped forward into the doorway and caught the gang boss with the gun broken and two fresh cartridges in his hand.

Radd threw down the shotgun and lifted a pistol from the bed. Hart shook his head and triggered his Colt. Two shots struck Radd's already bandaged chest. The gang boss slipped sideways and lay motionless as he relaxed into death, his narrowed eyes staring sightlessly at the man who had killed him. The wounded outlaw beside the bed was unconscious.

Hart heard the sound of hoofs outside and crossed to the window to peer out. The guard was fleeing as fast as his horse could travel. Hart lowered his deadly gun, his mind ticking over as he considered the situation. He had a feeling that it was all done, and gazed at the dead gang boss while he reloaded his smoking gun. Already his mind was composing a report for Captain Buckbee.

We do hope that you have enjoyed reading this large print book.

Did you know that all of our titles are available for purchase?

We publish a wide range of high quality large print books including:
Romances, Mysteries, Classics
General Fiction
Non Fiction and Westerns

Special interest titles available in large print are:
The Little Oxford Dictionary
Music Book, Song Book
Hymn Book, Service Book

Also available from us courtesy of Oxford University Press:
Young Readers' Dictionary
(large print edition)
Young Readers' Thesaurus
(large print edition)

For further information or a free brochure, please contact us at:
Ulverscroft Large Print Books Ltd.,
The Green, Bradgate Road, Anstey,
Leicester, LE7 7FU, England.
Tel: (00 44) **0116 236 4325**
Fax: (00 44) **0116 234 0205**

Other titles in the
Linford Western Library:

HAL GRANT'S WAR

Elliot James

When Hal Grant's father was bushwhacked in the street, it was the opening shot of a range war. Wealthy ranchers were determined to rid Lundon County of its sharecroppers and sodbusters eking out an existence in the marginal lands. Hal should have sided with his fellow ranchers, but he did not believe in mob law. He was caught in the middle — and no one was allowed to sit on the fence in a conflagration that was consuming a county . . .

THEY CALLED HIM LIGHTNING

Mark Falcon

A blow to the head had caused him memory loss and temporary blindness. Was he Mike Clancey, the name inscribed on the pocket watch he carried? And the beautiful woman's picture on the inside of the watch — was she his wife? He needed answers. Known as Lightning for his gun skills, riding Thunder, a black gelding, with fair play and talent he would bring a tyrant to justice — but it was a dangerous trail he must follow.